# Expectation of Pain

# Expectation of Pain

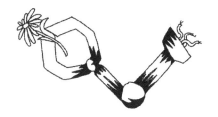

Above the Rain Collective

2024

Above the Rain Collective
abovetheraincollective@gmail.com
North Georgia, USA

Contributing Editor: J.A. Sexton

Publisher's note:

This is a work of fiction. All characters and incidents are the product of the author's imagination, places are used fictitiously and any resemblance to an actual person, living or dead, is entirely coincidental.

ISBN: 979-8-9899186-3-8

First Printing October 2024

abovetheraincollective.com
authorjulietrose.com

Cover graphics and interior formatting by J.A. Sexton
Above the Rain Collective logo artwork and original cover/chapter art by Bee Freitag

*For Octavia Butler*

# Chapter One

*I*shi pushed the rotten potato around the cracked plate with his fork. He glanced at the doorway, hoping Ms. Virginia wasn't watching. While he was hungry, the violent vomiting the food gave him last time was causing him pause. Stomach pains because of hunger or stomach pains because of food poisoning?

He'd take the chance on hunger. That was the safer bet. After all, last time, the vomiting caused severe dehydration and he almost didn't make it through.

"You need to toughen up, boy," Ms. Virginia had told him, as she eyed his crumpled form lying in sweat and puke on the soiled mattress. "You sure are fortunate to have me, you'd be dead on the streets without my care."

Ishi had kept his eyes squeezed shut but knew no response would end with him in the hole. The hole being just that. A hole deep in the basement where errant children were put for punishment.

He summoned all his strength and murmured, "Thank you, Ms. Virginia."

"That's right," she hurumphed and turned on her heel, shifting her massive body through the doorway. She stroked the large toad perched on her shoulder and muttered soft, loving sentiments to its wet and bumpy body. The toad she called Seoul received a gentle and delicate hand from Ms. Virginia, while the children there on the island received reproach and at times, a heavy hand. Seoul served another purpose to her, as he secreted a substance she often made challenging children drink. This made them quiet and subservient. Sometimes it made them go crazy, seeing things that weren't there.

Ishi couldn't remember a time not living on the island. When he asked Ms. Virginia where he came from, she shrugged and smiled in a way that made him feel she might eat him. "No one wanted you, with your leg all twisted up like that. All of you children are throwaways. Unwanted, a nuisance. Lucky for you, I came along and took you under my wing."

Under her wing. Ishi didn't know a different life but if it was worse than being under Ms. Virginia's wing, he was terrified of it. So he kept his head down, did his chores, and tried his best to be compliant. That's what she wanted, compliance.

Unquestioning obedience.

In addition to Ms. Virginia, Seoul, and the children, the island was inhabited by a slew of robots. They took care of the tasks the children didn't, or couldn't, and at Ms. Virginia's bidding, kept the children in line. It wasn't unheard of to be dragged out of bed and given "treatments" by the robots.

Treatments were whatever Ms. Virginia came up with to punish the children.

Ishi rubbed the scars on his arms and shuddered, remembering the last treatment he'd received, a series of burns and shocks. Most times, the children had no idea what they'd done to receive the punishment, but that time Ms. Virginia observed and when it was done, told a shaking Ishi, "Stop asking stupid questions."

Ishi stopped asking, though his mind was always wondering, always searching. Where did he come from? Why was he thrown away? He stared at his twisted left leg, a large healed wound running from top to bottom. The leg was almost immobile, however, with a gnarled walking cane, he managed to get around. To do his chores.

On the island, chores consisted of simple things like cleaning and cooking to more difficult tasks like moving boulders and chopping down trees. Good children were allowed "art" time but had to do whatever was on the schedule that day. It could be twelve hours of making wooden dolls or carving bowls out of the trees they chopped down. Their hands would blister and bleed, but it was still better than being outside doing manual labor for twelve hours. At least during art time, they got to sit most of the time. Once they were done, they were sent to their space, never seeing their projects again.

Ishi learned at a very young age to behave, so he could do art time. His leg prevented him from chopping too many trees or moving rocks, and if he didn't accomplish a certain amount of tasks a day, he'd receive treatments for his failures.

After stuffing the rotten potato in his waistband, he stood up and washed his plate in the basin. Washed probably wasn't the right term, as the water was oily and brown. The plate came out greasier than it went in. He sighed and stuck it on the stack of plates next to the basin, all of them covered in the oily substance.

He made his way to to art room and sat down. If they weren't eating or sleeping or doing schoolwork, they were working. Other children filtered in, their heads low as they took their places. They didn't dare speak to one another and saved that for late at night when Ms. Virginia went to bed. Ishi picked up the doll's head he was working on and let it roll around his palm. Toys weren't something they had on the island, but he couldn't deny he was drawn to the blue-eyed, blond-haired doll. It seemed happy.

Once the children were gathered, Ms. Virginia came in, stroking Seoul on the head. She glared around the room, her thin lips twisted in disgust. She eyed Ishi, however, he was smart enough to drop his eyes. He was the oldest child on the island, not that it meant much in his day-to-day life. What he did know, is once children got to be a certain age, they were taken elsewhere. At sixteen.

Adult-sized.

Ishi was now as tall as Ms. Virginia. He was almost sixteen.

A robot came into the room, leading a young girl. The robots all looked different and some were in a state of disrepair. Missing arms, rusting. Occasionally, a new one would show up, but Ishi recognized parts of them from different robots. Like they were cannibalized into a new machine. It seemed to make them angry, resentful, and they took it out on the children. Well, not all of them. Each robot had varying degrees of behavior, ranging from disinterest to cruelty. Ishi assumed it came from Ms. Virginia's treatment of them, as well.

Sometimes, he'd find robot parts scattered in the woods. He noticed the other robots would pause at the discarded parts, often picking up pieces and carrying them with them. They seemed sad when they did this, holding the scattered parts close to where their hearts would be if they had hearts.

The robot leading the girl, though, was one Ishi didn't mind being around. He was never cruel and often stepped in to help the children when they were struggling to move boulders. His name was Oslo and he tended to stay in the back, letting larger robots lead the way. He was smaller than most of the other robots, standing at Ishi's height. The bigger robots pushed him aside. Oslo let them, hovering around the children as they worked.

The girl trembled and Ms. Virginia led her to the front of the room, her fingers digging into the girl's thin shoulders. Not just thin, she appeared as if she was made of skin and bone. Her eyes were sunken, her lips cracked and dry. Ishi watched from the corner of his eye, knowing any direct eye contact with Ms. Virginia could lead to more treatments. Ms. Virgina cleared her throat, a wet raspy sound.

"Children, we have another member added to our family. I, again, came to the rescue of this poor child whose mother threw her away like trash. She has come to our sanctuary, and isn't she lucky she did? Now, Jai, go over and sit by Ishi, he can show you what to do. Ishi, raise your hand so Jai knows where to sit. I expect you'll teach her how to make the dolls. No chit-chat or I'll need to deal with you both."

"Yes, Ma'am," Ishi replied, raising his hand, but keeping his eyes down.

Jai stumbled as she made her way to sit next to him, her bones jutting out of her face. She looked like a skeleton, yet she was alive.

Once Ms. Virginia left, Oslo stayed and watched over the children. Ishi showed Jai how to assemble the wooden dolls and paint their faces. He wanted to ask her so many questions since she came to the island older than the rest of them. He'd been brought there as a toddler, not remembering life outside. Jai shook and dropped the doll, her fingers frozen in a claw. Ishi scooped it up, handing it back to her.

"Are you okay?"

She nodded, her attention fixed on the doll's blue eyes staring back at her. She started to waver and Ishi thought she might pass out. He put his arm around her shoulders to keep her upright and whispered, "Have you eaten recently?"

Jai shook her head. Ishi fished the potato out of his waistband and held it out to her. "It's not good. Don't eat the black parts."

She snatched it from him and shoved it in her mouth, ignoring what he'd told her. Ishi hoped it wouldn't make her sick, but she needed to eat before she passed out. He took the doll she was supposed to be working on and finished it quickly. They had a quota to meet and if they didn't, Ms. Virginia would order treatments.

Oslo watched the pair from the front of the room, his green, round eyes seeming almost curious. Ishi sucked in his breath and realized his error. The children were not allowed to help one another if they were struggling. Ms. Virginia said struggling built character. Ishi focused on his work, glancing up at Oslo. Oslo continued to observe them, then did something Ishi wasn't expecting. Oslo raised his metal hand and acted like he was locking a lock with a key in front of his mouth. A gesture that said so much to Ishi.

He wouldn't tell.

See, not only did the older children and robots disappear at times. Sometimes, in the middle of the night, a child would be taken away for a treatment. Usually, a child who challenged Ms. Virginia or broke a rule.

Except, they never came back.

# Chapter Two

The children were separated into areas by gender except during schooling or chores, so Ishi didn't get a chance to talk to Jai until they ended up on kitchen duty together about a month later. Ishi got kitchen duty a lot due to his leg and mobility limitations.

All of the children had some form of limitation but most could still work the fields and do manual labor. Ishi could, as well, however, Ms Virginia complained about his speed and said she preferred him in the kitchen. He suspected it was because he could actually cook. Well... when there was food to cook. Most times it was lard, potatoes, and wilted fruit and vegetables. No, not wilted. Rotten. He preferred to cook because he made sure to cook the food to excess, so they didn't get sick.

The last time he got sick, he'd been assigned to the laundry and Ms. Virginia had the robots cook. They had no idea what they were doing. He tried to give them instructions but most of the robots were mean, brusk. Oslo was the only one he honestly liked.

Speaking of Oslo, the mismatched robot was already in the kitchen when Ishi came in for his shift. The robot had his head down and was attempting to cut potatoes with his fingered hand. The other arm had a clamp that didn't serve much purpose. Ishi could relate as he moved his mangled leg around the table to help Oslo. Oslo glanced over, one of his round, glass eyes burnt out.

"Oslo, what happened to your eye?" Ishi asked as he took the knife from the robot.

Oslo blinked his other eye and tipped his head. "I do not know. It went out. Ms. Virginia said I do not need it."

Ms Virginia was like that. Ishi remembered asking her about his leg when he was a small child and she'd shrugged. Her answer was even less compassionate.

"You're broken, boy. Be glad I came along or they would've thrown you in the ditch for the dogs to eat."

Ishi didn't know what a dog was, but he pictured a large, ferocious beast with claws and gnashing teeth. He never asked again. After all, she never really answered the question, anyway. None of the children seemed to know how or why they ended up on the island and Ms. Virginia at best was dismissive. At worst, she was cruel. As Ishi noted, children disappeared all the time. The older ones once they turned sixteen, others randomly never showed back up.

Jai came into the kitchen with her head down. She was still rail-thin and her coloring was off. She briefly met Ishi's stare, then set to pulling vegetables out of a basket she was carrying. She cut the black spots off, then scraped off the slimy

15

coating the vegetables always seemed to have. Ishi handed Oslo a pot to start boiling potatoes and went over to Jai.

"Do you want my help?" he asked the frail girl.

She glanced up at him, then at the door. "Are you allowed to?"

Ishi shrugged. "I guess. We'll make quick work of it. Ms. Virginia is taking her afternoon nap, so I think we'll be fine. Here, hand me that pile of greenies."

They didn't know what half the things they ate were, but they knew their colors. Jai slid them over and Ishi got to peeling off the rotten skin. Underneath was squishy yellow material. He sniffed it and began to cut it into circles. Jai watched him for a moment before setting her focus on a pile of red spheres. She pointed her knife at the greenies.

"Zucchini."

Ishi frowned. "What?"

"Those are called zucchini. These red round things are radishes."

Ishi was mesmerized. "How do you know that?"

Jai cocked her head, then scratched her chin. "I don't know, I just do. That's what we called them back home."

"Home? Where you came from?"

Jai nodded, then teared up, shifting her attention back to her work. "Yes."

"Where is home? Is it near the island?"

She set down her knife and sighed much too maturely for a girl of her age. "No. It's in the Western territories. Do you know where that is?"

Ishi didn't. Ms. Virginia spoke of the world outside of the island in general terms. She said it was a dark and evil place where people killed babies and hated each other. Ishi rolled the zucchini between his fingers and chewed his lip. "I've been here almost my whole life. I've only been on the island as long as I can remember."

Jai scowled and stared at him. "You don't remember your family?"

"You do?"

She peered out the window like she was expecting someone to show up. "I do. It was me and my mother."

Mother. It was a word Ishi rarely heard and when Ms. Virginia spoke it, she said it with disdain. He inherently knew he had a mother but it was forbidden to speak about, so he never asked about her. He focused on Jai. "You have a mother? Where is she? Why are you here?"

At this, Jai burst into tears and ran out of the room. Not wanting her to get in trouble for not completing her chores, Ishi stepped over and finished cutting her vegetables. Oslo was observing from across the room, then stepped over to Ishi's side.

"Her mother hurt her. Starved her. Ms. Virginia said she rescued her," his metallic voice explained.

"Hurt her? Why would a mother do that?" Ishi asked.

Oslo looked blankly at him and didn't respond. How could he? Robots didn't have mothers and Ms. Virginia was all they knew. Ishi tried to imagine what Jai's mother could have done to her as he finished prepping the food. Everything was thrown into the large pot and set to boil to ensure it killed anything that could make them sick.

A little while later, Jai came back in and glanced around. Ishi was washing dishes and Oslo was mopping. She picked up a rag and began wiping the tables down. As she came close to Ishi, she reached out and touched his arm.

"I'm sorry."

"For what? I'm sorry for making you cry."

"For not helping cook. I'm still having a hard time."

Ishi turned to face her and frowned. "I've been here my whole life. I don't remember my mother or anything else. Ms. Virginia said they would've thrown me in the ditch. I guess she's right with my ugly leg."

Jai stared at his leg, then shook her head. "It's not ugly. But maybe she's right. There aren't kids like you where I come from. My... my mother wasn't well. She was for most of my life, but the last couple of years she forgot about me. To feed me, that I was even there. She never left bed except to perform. When she did perform, sometimes she'd leave and not come back for a long time. The school called The Guard enforcement and they showed up at the house. My mother had been gone a long time. I was sick... dizzy and weak. My mother had locked me in a closet, so I couldn't escape. They told me I had to go with them to a halfway house. From there, Ms. Virginia took me in."

Ishi listened in fascination. He wanted to ask her more questions about where she came from, but the food was ready and he could hear Ms. Virginia moving through the halls. He quickly shut off the pot off and began scooping the hot mixture into bowls. Jai carried the bowls out to the cafeteria and set them on tables. Ms. Virginia came into the cafeteria and watched her. Jai kept her head down, then went back into the kitchen. She and Ishi worked silently as they served the rest of the food.

After they finished bringing the food to the cafeteria, Ishi turned to Jai. "How old are you?"

"Eleven."

He was surprised. Based on her size, he thought her to be only about nine years old. He carried the trash can out as they were leaving and turned to her. "I'm fifteen."

Jai turned her head and narrowed her eyes. "Why aren't there any older kids here? Like older than you?"

Ishi set the trash can down and adjusted his walking stick to get a better grip. "I don't know. They leave when they turn sixteen. Maybe they go back to their home?"

Jai considered this, then shook her head. "No. Because there aren't people like you where I came from. You know... like different? All the kids here are different."

"Maybe they go to another island, then," Ishi answered with irritation. He knew they didn't in his heart but didn't like to consider the other possibilities. He thought about the robot pieces in the woods. Ms. Virginia didn't like it when she couldn't control things.

Oslo came up behind them and held the door so Ishi could get through with the trash can. Ishi turned to him.

"Oslo, what happens to kids here when they turn sixteen?"

Oslo didn't meet his eyes and kept his head down. Impatient, Ishi used his elbow to get Oslo's attention. "Oslo?"

The robot lifted his head, his one dark eye creating an uncomfortable void. "Ms Virginia sells them."

Sells them? What did that even mean? Ishi looked at Jai and her expression said she knew. He knew he wouldn't get more out of Oslo, so he shifted his attention to her.

"What does that mean? Sells them?"

Jai shook her head and muttered, "Nothing good."

Before he could press her further, Ms Virginia came around the corner and glared at the three of them in the doorway. "It takes three of you to take out the trash?"

Jai scurried down the hall to the cafeteria and Oslo let the door go as Ishi gripped the can. Without looking back, Oslo disappeared in the other direction, leaving Ishi and Ms. Virginia standing face to face. She reached up and rubbed the toad on her shoulder as she watched Ishi, unblinking.

"What were you all talking about, instead of working?" she asked, her voice rigid.

"Nothing, Ms. Virginia. I was telling Jai she needed to gather up any remaining bowls and wash them," Ishi lied.

Ms Virginia stared at him, then laughed. "See, the older you all get, the more sneaky you children get. That's why I don't like the older children being here. They cause trouble and have to go. Which reminds me, Ishi."

Ishi waited and when she didn't speak, he cleared his throat, setting down the heavy trash at his feet. His stomach twisted in knots as he very much felt like an animal in a trap. "Reminds you of what, Ms. Virginia?"

She smiled an extremely unhappy, yet intentional, smile and winked at him. "Your upcoming birthday."

# Chapter Three

The incessant beeping woke Ishi and he sat up in bed, rubbing the sleep from his eyes. It was an alarm. The children were only allowed to trip it in an emergency. He swung his legs out of bed and peered around. Or tried to. It was pitch black and only the sliver of moonlight coming through the window offered any light.

"Hello?" he called out in the dark. Something wasn't right. Usually, the robots were around guarding over them in the night.

Ishi fished for his walking stick, remembering he'd left it in the hall closet. That was the requirement of the children. They weren't allowed to bring anything to bed with them. Not even their support equipment. If they needed something in the night, they were to call on the robots. They weren't even allowed to use the bathroom after the lights went out. He sighed and groped for the bed rail to stand up. A small voice across the large room got his attention.

"I need help."

"Darius? Is that you?" Ishi spoke to the sound.

"Yes. I am not well."

Ishi frowned. Where were the robots? Why was it so dark? He stood and moved along the wall to Darius's bed. The small boy was only eight years old and blind since birth. He got to Darius's bed and sat down next to the boy.

"What's going on? Are you sick?"

"Yes. I need to go to the bathroom. I triggered the alarm but no one came. I don't have my stick."

Ishi took Darius's hand and rose. "I don't know what's going on, but I can try to help. Can you make it to the bathroom?"

"I think so. I need to throw up."

At that, Ishi started leading the way across the black room, smacking his knees painfully against bed frames as he attempted to find the door. Other boys stirred but no one rose to help. Ishi knew they were afraid of getting in trouble with Ms. Virginia.

Ms. Virginia.

She'd pulled him aside about his birthday but the conversion had been odd. She told him it was time for him to move to an adult camp once he turned sixteen. However, the more he asked her about it, the less information she gave. By the time they were done talking, he was more confused than ever. She'd stared off with an odd smile on her face. Like she was the cat who ate the canary. It scared him and he wished he wouldn't turn sixteen. Even though life on the island was tough, he at least knew what to expect. He had no idea what an adult camp was or what he was supposed to do there.

They found the doorway and Ishi stepped through it, noting the hallway was pitch black and no robots were around. They inched along the outer wall toward the bathroom, passing the girls' room. It was also devoid of light and no sound or movement came from it.

Ishi was frightened and called out. "Oslo? Are you around?"

Silence greeted him and he clasped Darius's hand even tighter. As they were nearing the bathroom, Ishi tumbled over something hard and cold, landing face-first on the floor. He lost his grip on Darius, but not before yanking the boy on top of him. Pain shot through Ishi's head and he struggled to get out from under the child.

"Ow! What did I trip over?" he mumbled, using his hands to feel around. They landed on metal and he moved his hands over the shape to determine what it was. Oslo. But he wasn't moving.

Darius began to cry loudly, and Ishi shifted his focus to the boy. "Are you alright?"

Darius hiccuped and reached out for Ishi. "I cut my leg when I fell on that thing. What is it?"

"It's Oslo, but he's... um, I guess turned off."

"Off?"

"Like not working. The power is out, too, so maybe it affected the robots," Ishi explained.

"Should we get Ms. Virginia?" Darius asked.

"Do you *want* to get Ms. Virginia?" Ishi responded, not as a question, rather as a warning.

Darius was quiet for a moment, then whispered, "No. That would be bad."

Ishi helped them both up and pushed the bathroom door open, guiding Darius to a toilet. "Here, reach out and you can feel the rim. I'll keep an eye out."

Darius did as he was told and just in time, as vomit began spewing out of his small frame. Ishi hoped it all landed in the toilet because Ms. Virginia would cane them if it didn't. Ishi swallowed hard when he smelled the vomit and held his breath. It wasn't uncommon for the children to get sick with the quality of food they were eating, however, this smelled worse. Like illness or food poisoning. A shudder ran through him for Darius. There were no doctors on the island. If they got sick, Ms. Virginia made them wait it out. If they recovered, they were right back to work the next day. If they didn't, they were never seen or heard from again.

Darius fell to his knees and wept. He too knew he needed to get better on his own. Ishi racked his brain, trying to think of a way to help the trembling boy. The children figured things out over the years to treat what they could, but it helped to know what they were dealing with. This could be anything. Food poisoning, virus, infection.

Ishi sat next to Darius and cradled the child in his arms. "How long have you been sick?"

"Since this morning," came the weak answer.

"Did you eat something that made you sick?"

"I don't think so. I woke up sick and hid it, so I didn't get a beating."

Ishi understood. Not only did Ms. Virginia make them deal with it on their own, she had them beaten for getting sick. He rubbed Darius's back and sighed. "It's alright Dari, we'll get you through this. Is this the first time you vomited?"

"No, I vomited after dinner, too. It's getting worse, like rats are chewing on my stomach."

They were all too familiar with the rats and what they could do. They infested the island and came into the children's rooms. Ishi often had to flick rat droppings off the food he was preparing. He rubbed his temple and thought.

"Did you sneak food?"

By Darius's silence, he knew the answer. Ishi always made sure the food he prepared was free of rat droppings and cooked to kill any bacteria, however, the children were so hungry, occasionally one would get desperate and steal food.

Dari went rigid and sniffled. "Don't tell. Please, don't tell on me, Ishi."

"I won't but, Dari, you can't take food. It needs to be inspected and cooked, so you don't get sick."

"Ishi, I'm so hungry. I can't sleep because my belly hurts all the time from being empty."

Ishi knew the feeling all too well. While they were given food, it was often rotten and never enough. Children wasted away, often until they simply vanished in the night. He couldn't blame the boy but knew Dari was taking his life in his hands by stealing food.

"I'll try to sneak you extra, but you can't take food anymore. It's not safe."

At that, Darius began puking again and Ishi held him, so he could direct it toward the toilet.

All of a sudden, the lights came on, flooding the area with a bright white glow. Ishi could see that, in fact, Dari had not gotten all of the vomit into the toilet and groaned inwardly. The floor was covered with the liquid. He needed to get that cleaned up before one of the robots informed Ms. Virginia and she beat them both.

Once Dari was finished with that round, Ishi got up and gathered rags from under the sink. He started wiping up the thick and sticky substance when he heard someone coming down the hall. Panic froze him, his hand clutching the rag in midair. Terrified, he turned his eyes to the door, waiting for the inevitable. He could almost feel the lashes against his leg.

When Jai appeared at the door, he almost cried in relief. She looked confused and stared between Darius and Ishi. "What are you doing?"

"Dari is sick. I'm helping him. The lights were off and no robots were around. He needed to throw up."

"Oh. Oslo is in the hallway but something is wrong with him. He is lying there and his eyes keep flashing on and off. I heard you talking and came to see what was happening. Is Dari alright?"

"I don't think so. He keeps vomiting. I think he ate tainted food. Here, come help. I'm trying to clean up around the toilet, so Ms. Virginia doesn't cane us," Ishi said, holding out a clean rag.

Jai came over and began wiping the floor with the rag, keeping her eyes on the door. In a few minutes, they had the space clean and it appeared Darius was done vomiting, though he was curled into a ball on the floor, whimpering. Ishi had seen it before and worry gnawed at his gut. He liked Dari, considered him a little brother. If he'd ever had a brother, he didn't remember. He'd read about siblings in the books they had for school and the idea intrigued him.

Family.

Jai grasped his arm, her eyes wide. Something was coming their way. Ishi began forming excuses in his head to explain why all three of them were out of bed. Darius being sick wasn't enough to keep them out of trouble. They weren't supposed to help each other. He stood and prepared for the worst to come.

Oslo came around the corner, his movements jerky and uncoordinated. His one eye was lit up, the other still out but flickering. He stared at the three children, assessing what he was seeing. Observing Darius curled up by the toilet, Oslo put it together. He came close and extended his one arm.

"You get back to bed." His words were fragmented but the children understood. He motioned to Jai and Ishi. "Go, now."

They knew he'd keep their secret safe and Ishi and Jai scuttled past him, back to their rooms before any other robots showed up. Ishi paused at the door as he watched Oslo gather Darius in his arms and limp toward the door with the boy.

Ishi climbed back into bed, after seeing Jai to her room. Oslo was not far behind, dragging one of his legs behind him. At that moment, Ishi felt a kinship with the robot and immense gratitude for Oslo's kindness. If robots could be kind. As Oslo tucked Darius into bed, other robots appeared in the hallway. Their movements were also off and Ishi realized the power outage had affected them, as well. They were trying to catch up with their systems.

One of the robots Ishi didn't care for, Moscow, stood in the doorway, watching Oslo with Darius. Though Ms. Virginia said the robots couldn't feel or express emotions, Ishi could swear Moscow seemed irritated. When Oslo went to go out of the door, the larger robot refused to move. Oslo dropped his head and waited. After a bit, Moscow spun and disappeared down the hall.

Oslo turned and stared at Ishi, a look that could only pass for sadness crossed his face and he glanced at Darius, his other eye beginning to flicker on more consistently. Ishi knew. Dari was in bad shape. He probably wouldn't survive and like the others before him, would be gone one morning, never to be seen again.

Ishi met Oslo's eyes and for the first time ever, he wasn't willing to sit idly by and allow another child to be taken by the night. As if words traveled in silence between them, Ishi understood Oslo felt the same. Oslo nodded slightly and left the room.

Ishi finally had someone on his side.

# Chapter Four

The following morning, Ishi rose with the sun and checked on Darius before the robots woke the other children. Dari was sweating and pale, huddled in his thin blanket in the fetal position. Ishi glanced toward the door, considering what to do. Dari was already too thin and couldn't risk losing any more weight. Setting his mind to doing something he wasn't allowed to, he slipped into the hall, peering in both directions.

Seeing the coast was clear, he darted to the kitchen and closed the door behind him. He rummaged through the cabinets, pulling out supplies. He'd make a broth for Dari to hopefully replenish the salt and liquid the boy had lost. Ishi kept the lights off and did his best to make a nutritious and palatable mixture. It wasn't much, but Darius needed to keep something down to ward off dehydration.

As he was stirring the concoction on the stove, Ishi heard movement outside the kitchen door and dread set in. He grasped the pot, shoving it into the oven before the door swung open. Relief washed over him when he saw it was Oslo, though he still didn't totally trust the robot. He couldn't. Ms. Virginia controlled them all. Oslo came in, one of his eyes still dimmer than the other, limping on his mismatched legs.

"Uh, hey, Oslo. I was just getting a jump start on breakfast," Ishi stammered.

Oslo observed Ishi and shut the kitchen door behind him, which surprised Ishi. There was a very strict rule that no doors were to be shut by the children or robots. Ishi waited, his heart pounding in his chest. Oslo moved to the other side of the long metal table between them and stood quietly, gazing at Ishi. His dimmed eye gave him an unhinged look. He gestured to the oven.

"You cannot hide the smell," the robot said, his voice just above a whisper.

Could robots smell?

Ishi shifted uncomfortably. "I didn't think about that. It's for Dari, he's weak."

Oslo put his fingered hand out. "I will give it to him."

Ishi felt like he was being set up and frowned. Was Oslo going to dump the mixture and tell Ms. Virginia? Ishi stood frozen, his mind turning over what he was facing. "Darius needs it."

Oslo reached his arm further toward Ishi and bobbed his head. "I will bring it to him, so you do not get caught and end up in trouble."

Ishi was floored. He'd always liked Oslo but this was a side of him he didn't expect. "Oslo, what happened last night? Why did the power go out?"

Oslo's head dipped slightly and he glanced at the door. Seeing no one was coming, he lifted his head to Ishi, his straight mouth seeming to form a grimace. "Raiders."

"Raiders? What does that mean?"

"Humans came to the island. They cut the power sources and tried to scale the walls of the house."

Ishi was both horrified and intrigued. Why would anyone want to come to the island to get into the compound? Every night, the compound was locked up from the inside and no one was allowed out or in. Who were these humans? Were they after the children? He cleared his throat and pulled the pot out of the oven, pouring some of the mixture into a mug for Dari.

"Why were they here? What happened to them?"

Oslo reached for the mug and met Ishi's eyes. "I do not know. Ms. Virginia says they want the island, want to destroy us all. They were not able to get through the razor wire before the power was restored."

Ishi had so many questions but wanted Oslo to get the broth to Dari before anyone else came around. Frustrated, he peered at the door. "Who restored the power?"

Oslo shrugged, clutching the mug. "Generator."

There was a backup generator to run the computer systems. Ms. Virginia must've turned it on when she saw the power was out. That would have repowered the robots, who then fought back the humans. Or so Ishi gathered. Oslo went to the door and Ishi needed to know one more thing before he left.

"Oslo, do you believe Ms. Virginia? Do you think the humans were here to hurt us?"

Oslo didn't turn, but Ishi heard his soft response loud and clear. Oslo pushed the door open, balancing the mug in his claw hand. He paused and did something very human.

He sighed at the question and whispered, "No."

That was it, nothing more was said. Oslo slipped out of the door, heading to the boys' room and Darius. It was in the robot's hands now. Ishi could hear activity in the hallway and children moving to their stations. He began making breakfast, glad to find some not rotten potatoes and onions. He was surprised to find a small packet of meat and used it to flavor the hash he was making.

They almost never got meat and didn't know what the occasion was. He was smart enough not to question it, or ask for more, and got to work.

By the time breakfast was done and the dishes washed, Ishi was ready to move to his next task. He was to strip all the boys' bedding and wash it in the laundry room. It was his chore once a week and he dreaded it as carrying the heavy loads took its toll on his leg. However, today he was glad for it, so he could check in on Dari.

Ishi stepped into the hall and saw Jai carrying a load of the girls' bedding. He was happy to be working with her today as they never had a chance to talk. He was intrigued by the only child he knew who came to the island with memories of the outside world and wanted to know more.

As he stripped the bedding, he made sure to do it so he could repeatedly circle around to Dari and check on him. He pressed his hand against the sleeping boy's head and was relieved there was no fever. Dari hadn't thrown up recently, either. That was a good sign. The boy was twitchy and sleeping, so Ishi let him be. He shoved a clean set of sheets under the mattress to change later, once Darius was awake.

In the laundry room, Jai was shoving sheets into the washer. Too many and unbalanced, so Ishi stepped over to assist her. He smiled and removed half the sheets, sorting the rest to either side.

"This way the washer won't get off-kilter, making a bunch of noise. Ms. Virginia gets angry when that happens," he explained.

"Don't want to make her highness mad," Jai muttered with a level of venom in her voice Ishi wasn't expecting.

He suppressed a laugh and glanced at the door. "Shhh, you'll get a beating for that if anyone hears you."

Jai shrugged. "Can't be worse than what my mother did to me."

"You mean starving you?"

Jai met his eyes, her own dark and wary. "Yeah. She locked me in the closet and didn't feed me on purpose. When The Guard came and found me like that, they took me away."

Ishi had always dreamed his mother was out there somewhere, searching for him. He couldn't imagine a mother could be so cruel. "Why did she do that?"

Jai didn't reply and turned to the washer, setting the dial. Ishi loaded another washer, afraid to ask any more questions. Jai moved to sort the sheets into smaller piles and worked silently. Ishi could see her shoulders shaking and realized she was crying. He wanted to comfort her, but it was strictly forbidden.

As they moved the sheets to the dryers since it was raining out, Jai turned to him. "My mother was two people.

My mother and what I called 'the rage'. I never knew who she'd be when I woke up. As the years went on, she became more and more rage and less and less of my mother."

Ishi didn't know what to say and simply listened. Jai rubbed her nose, staring out of the window. She took in a deep, shuddering breath and faced him.

"She tried to kill me one night. Came into my room and tried to stab me. My screams were the only thing that stopped her. After that, she locked me in the closet. School is mandatory, so they came looking for me."

"Did she get in trouble?"

Jai shook her head. "No. My mother is famous."

Ishi had no clue what famous meant and frowned at her. "What's that?"

"A lot of people know who she is. She is a singer and performs for people. Lots of people. So, they took me away, instead. Made me disappear."

"That's why you are here?" Ishi asked.

"Yes. They told me I was a bad girl and needed to go where all the other unwanted, trash children went."

Unwanted, trash children? Ms. Virginia always said the children came there because they didn't have families, but Jai did. She had a *famous* mother who didn't want her. Did Ishi have a family that didn't want him, as well? Jai was the key to the outside world and he wanted to know everything. He was just about to ask her about the world outside the island when one of the robots came into the laundry room and observed them from the door. They weren't supposed to be talking and got caught.

No more questions were going to be asked.

They each finished their loads and took them back to the rooms to remake the beds. Ishi's brain was running over their conversation. He needed to know more. He'd begun to wonder the older he got about what was really out there. However, once he turned sixteen, he'd be shuttled off to the adult camp on another island, or so Ms. Virginia said. He wasn't sure he believed her and feared for the future.

At dinner that evening, Ishi was relieved to see Darius in his weakened state, sitting at a table with Oslo. Ishi sat across from them and slid a piece of paper he tore from a book to Oslo. Ishi wasn't sure the robot could read, but he needed to take the chance. Oslo used a tray to move the paper closer, then tucked it into his mouth.

One thing Ms. Virginia insisted on, was educating the children. Once a month, a man came to the island with an electronic machine and took notes. He asked the children questions about math, language, and geography. He'd have them write an essay about something random. Maybe about plants or the sky. Things like that. He'd read the essays and make more notes on the device. Ishi never really understood, but those days they were required to bathe and wear their "Sunday clothes" as Ms. Virginia referred to them. The children were to only answer questions asked of them and say nothing more. The man never seemed concerned about anything more than their studies, anyway. Not even when children were missing.

If they dared say anything else, they were caned or given treatments when the man left. Ishi assumed they were educated to meet the man's questions and that was all. He had a lot of knowledge about nothing important. He could read, write, repeat times tables, and point to territories on a map. He wasn't sure why any of it was important when all he did was cook and clean all day. However, he was grateful, either way.

It was the only way he could communicate with the robot, who he hoped would keep his secret safe and find a way to help him. To create a line of communication with Jai.

His life depended on it.

# Chapter Five

Before he could understand what was happening, Ishi was dragged out of bed and down the hall, the cruel hand of Moscow pulling him by his shirt. Ishi tried to break free, but the robot only held tighter. Ishi squinted past the bright ceiling lights to see where he was being taken, though, in his heart, he knew. His knees banged painfully against the floor as he was shuttled down the narrow hall.

As suspected, he was brought to Ms. Virginia's door and tossed unceremoniously against the wall. The door flew open and another robot rushed out, shoving Jai in front of it. She was crying and from the angry welts across her legs, she'd received a vicious caning. Jai averted her eyes as they passed Ishi, her mouth set in a tight line. Ishi was forced up and through the doorway to come face to face with Ms. Virginia. Seoul, the toad, sat on her desk, his eyes flat. He almost looked like a statue except for the random times his tongue flicked out of his mouth.

Ishi stared at Ms. Virginia, who was red and sweaty, clutching the cane in her hand. He braced himself for the beating and hoped Jai was spared the worst of Ms. Virginia's wrath. Instead, much to his surprise, she set the cane down next to Seoul and glared at Ishi.

"You know better."

Ishi nodded. He did. He and Jai were caught conversing and that was an infraction that came with heavy consequences. Even though she'd set it down, he couldn't take his eyes off the cane, already feeling its sting against his legs and back. Ms. Virginia moved to the other side of the desk and heaved herself into the creaky wooden chair. She motioned for Ishi to sit down. When he didn't move, Moscow shoved him into the adjacent chair. Ishi tried to make himself as small as possible.

Ms. Virginia leaned back, eyeing him. "See, this is why children are sent away at sixteen. They become a bad influence. You made me beat that child. She sure did scream and holler."

Ishi felt guilt wash across him, his cheeks flaming. "I'm sorry, Ms. Virginia. She didn't deserve it, you should have only caned me."

Her eyes narrowed as rage set across her thick jowls. "How dare you tell me what I should do!" she screamed. "Don't you ever speak like that to me."

Ishi recognized his mistake and hung his head. "Sorry, Ms. Virginia."

She took a deep breath and flicked her hand for Moscow to leave. "It's a shame, you were a good cook. However, you have proven you can't be trusted. I've arranged your transport to the adult camp for the end of the week. You turn sixteen the day after, however, the trip takes many days. You'll be old enough when you arrive."

Ishi felt his heart drop. He was supposed to be there when he turned sixteen. To have a party, though, that just consisted of the children awkwardly singing *Happy Birthday* and being allowed one chocolate chip from Ms. Virginia's stash. Even so, Ishi wanted to be the with only family he knew. He began to speak, then saw Ms. Virginia's expression change and thought better of it. He was lucky she wasn't beating him at that moment, yet he still expected it coming.

Ms. Virginia stood up and came around the desk, grasping Ishi's face painfully in her hand. "You should be more grateful after all I did for you."

"Yes, Ms. Virginia," he muttered, trying to sound appreciative.

"Have your things packed by the end of the week. I'll let you say goodbye before you load on the boat."

Things. He didn't really have any except his issued gray cover-alls, shirts, pants, and his Sunday clothes. They weren't allowed personal effects. Against his better judgment, he asked, "What is the adult camp like? What will I do there?"

The slap came before he could move, stinging his eyes and leaving a throbbing handprint on his face. Ms. Virginia stepped back, her chest heaving with anger. "Did I say you could ask me questions? Insolent child!"

Ishi didn't dare answer. He pushed back the tears creeping their way out and considered the adult camp couldn't be worse than living under Ms. Virginia's rage. Could it? He waited for the caning, however, Ms. Virginia snapped her fingers and Moscow came back into the room. She motioned to

Ishi and Moscow yanked him out of the seat, dragging him back down the hallway. They passed Oslo, who looked away, avoiding Moscow's retaliation.

Ishi was thrown into the boys' room, sliding across the floor and landing against a bed frame. The child in it stirred and gazed in fear at the large robot. Realizing Moscow wasn't there for him, the boy quickly buried his head under his covers and turned away. Ishi gathered himself off the floor and made the way to his bed.

He glanced at Darius, who was facing him, his sightless eyes wide and afraid. Ishi tried to say something to him, but his mouth wouldn't move. He lifted his hand and touched Dari on the head, then hid his tears in his blanket. Who would watch over the younger ones once he was gone? No other children were close to Ishi's age, the nearest being twelve.

Ishi turned and tucked his head under his pillow, it was the only way he could feel more invisible. He had five days until he was sent away. To a new home. He couldn't picture what it looked like but hoped he would see some of the children, who'd left before when he arrived there. The ones he'd grown up with but had aged out of the island.

He heard crinkling across the room and sat up to see what it was. The boy, Jaroh, was eating something from a piece of paper. Ishi glanced at the door, then back at Jaroh. He was making too much noise, eating what was obviously stolen food. Ishi attempted to get his attention to have him quiet down but the boy was intent on scarfing down what was in the wrapper. The scent hit Ishi's nose and he shuddered. It wasn't food from the kitchen, it was some type of cured meat. Only Ms. Virginia had cured meat. Jaroh had stolen from Ms. Virginia!

One by one, the other boys woke up and stared over at Jaroh, who was now eating with abandon, the smell and noise filling the room. Ishi held his breath, wishing Jaroh would hurry up and finish before he was caught. The aroma was also making Ishi's stomach grumble. As Jaroh was getting to the last piece, Moscow appeared in the doorway. The boy and robot gazed at each other for a moment before it all set in. Then, as if in slow motion, Moscow crossed the room and snatched the last morsel of meat from Jaroh, holding it up. His other robot hand snaked out and grabbed Jaroh by the throat, lifting him out of bed.

Jaroh tried to scream and get loose, but Moscow's grip was too strong. He carried the boy in the air like a doll by his throat out of the room. The other boys could hear Jaroh screaming down the hall, his voice fading as they moved away. Ishi shivered, hoping Jaroh would only receive a caning and be brought back.

By morning, Jaroh still hadn't returned and Ishi knew he never would. The boys all dressed and made their beds in silence, their eyes darting to Jaroh's bed as they worked. They were used to children disappearing in the night, however, it never became less terrifying.

Ishi made his way to the kitchen, his legs and arms feeling rubbery. Why did Jaroh risk it when he knew the consequences? Why did he steal from Ms. Virginia, knowing her anger was unending? How did he even get into her space to take the food?

Ishi mulled all of this over as he worked. He was alone and lost in his thoughts when Oslo came in. Oslo waited for Ishi to realize he was there, standing by the door. When Ishi looked up, he was startled and dropped the bowl he was holding.

"Oslo, you scared me!"

Oslo came closer. "You must be more careful."

Ishi nodded. "Did you read my note?"

"Yes. You need my help."

The note had simply read, *Can you help me?*

"Yes," Ishi affirmed.

"How?" Oslo asked.

"Will you keep my secret, not tell anyone?" Ishi replied, hoping he could trust Oslo. It was his only chance.

"Yes."

"Can you find out about the adult camp? What it is like, what I'd be doing there?"

Oslo took a step back, his iridescent eyes catching the light. He bobbed his head and turned to leave. "I will try. Ishi, no more notes. No more talking. I will come to you if I find out anything."

After Oslo left, Ishi finished making breakfast and took it to the cafeteria on a rolling cart. He passed Moscow, who stared at him, waiting for Ishi to mess up. Ishi averted his eyes and pushed the cart faster. When he got to the cafeteria, he handed the cart off to a server and peered around the room. Darius wasn't there. Considering going back to the boys' quarters, Ishi stepped into the hallway. However, Moscow was lurking about and he knew he'd never make it to the boys' room without having to go past the hulking robot.

He stepped back into the cafeteria and sat down next to one of the younger boys. When no robots were looking, he leaned over to the boy.

"Where's Darius?"

The boy looked nervous. "He was taken to Ms. Virginia."

Ishi frowned. Darius hadn't done anything wrong. Not since he stole food from the kitchen, however, only Ishi knew about that. Well, Ishi and Jai. Jai. He stared around the room and caught her eye. She flushed red and looked down at her food. Ishi suspected she'd cracked when being caned and had given up Dari's name. He couldn't fault her but still, he was angry. And worried. Darius was recovering from being sick. He was a frail child, as well.

He might not survive one of Ms. Virginia's beatings. Ishi got up and made a terrible decision. He bolted for the door, intent on stopping Ms. Virginia from killing Darius. The other children sat with their mouths agape, knowing he was basically committing suicide. Ishi made it to the door and darted around Moscow, who had his back turned. He slipped past the giant robot and moved as fast as he could down the hallway.

He didn't see it coming when Oslo tackled him and dragged him down the hall, motioning to Moscow that he'd caught the errant child. Moscow glared, then rotated back to the cafeteria. Oslo gripped Ishi tight, making Ishi think he was being taken for a beating, then at the last second, tugged the boy into a dark room. Ishi frowned at the robot, not understanding when Oslo let him go, then shook his head.

"There is no adult camp."

# Chapter Six

Oslo's words rang in Ishi's ears, long after the robot guided him back to the room, so he wouldn't get in trouble. No adult camp. Ishi sat on the edge of his bed, remembering what Oslo told him. The older children, when they turned sixteen, didn't go to an adult camp. There was no better place.

"Where do they go, then?" Ishi asked the robot on the way to the room.

Oslo hadn't wanted to tell him at first, but Ishi insisted. After all, their fate would soon be his fate.

"They are sold to work camps."

"Work camps? Like here?"

Oslo had stared off, refusing to meet Ishi's eyes. "No, not like here. You work here, but Ms. Virginia has rules she has to follow. It is not like that at the work camps. No one survives those."

No one survives? How could that be?

"How do you know this?" Ishi asked, not wanting to know the answer.

"I clean Ms. Virginia's room every Thursday. I decided to look through her desk. I found..." the robot trailed off and stopped.

"Oslo? Found what? I need to know. Whatever you found impacts me. My future," Ishi insisted, trying to ignore the sweat forming on his palms.

"Ishi, I wish I had not seen what I did. There were files about past children. What happened to them."

"What happened to them?"

Oslo turned and met his eyes, his large round glowing orbs holding a sense of emotion robots didn't have. "They are sold to internment camps to work until they die. Which is not very long. Often, only months. Sometimes, they do not even make it there."

Ishi felt heat tingling through his body and recognized it as deep fear. "They kill them?"

Oslo turned away and shook his head. "They work them to death."

This couldn't be true! Why would they work them until they died, instead of keeping them around to work longer? "I don't understand. Why?"

"Ishi, they do not see the value of you children. You are broken to the world, worthless."

Ishi wanted to scream and yell, but Oslo would get in trouble. His mind wandered over the robot parts scattered in the woods, of the missing children over the years. They didn't have value.

"Then why does Ms. Virginia keep us around?"

"She gets paid to. The discards are paid for by the taxes where they came from. Per law, the government must pay for you until you turn sixteen. Then, you are supposed to be able to live out your days as workers."

"Discards? That's what they call us? Why?" Ishi knew Oslo's knowledge was limited and he was asking a question that didn't have a real answer.

"I do not know. However, Ms. Virginia gets a stipend for each of you children as long as you are educated and housed. That runs out at sixteen, so it seems she sells you to the work camps for a little extra."

"Why does the work camp not keep us around, working for the rest of our lives?" Theoretically, they did, even if the life was just a few months.

"You are considered worthless," Oslo said the words, but Ishi could tell the robot didn't agree with them.

Worthless. "Because of my leg? Because Darius is blind?"

Oslo rotated his head and if a robot could be sad, he certainly seemed to be. "Ishi, I am sorry. I am just telling you what I found."

Ishi bit back tears and nodded. "I know. Thank you for telling me. Where's Darius?"

"Ms. Virginia has him. She is not happy he is so weak. I heard her tell Moscow to take care of him tonight. To finalize his departure."

"Tonight?" Ishi exclaimed.

Children who departed never came back. They were seen without worth, not even for the stipend. Perhaps their upkeep cost more than Ms. Virginia thought it was worth. Ishi couldn't let anything happen to his little brother. He felt like he might vomit and leaned against the wall.

Oslo stopped and glanced up the hallway. "We must keep moving. I will tell Ms. Virginia you are sick and left the cafeteria to vomit. However, you are in serious danger."

Ishi knew. His birthday was the end of the week and he'd be sent away. To work to death. Darius wouldn't survive the night. He needed to do something.

As they made it to the boys' room, Ishi slowed his steps, thinking of anything else Oslo might know. He paused at the door and stared at the one being who he could trust.

"Oslo, does Ms. Virginia kill children here? The ones that never come back?"

Oslo tipped his head, his eyes growing dim. "Not with her own hands."

That was all the answer Ishi needed. She ordered the robots to, so she never had to get her hands dirty. "How does she explain that, to... to whoever pays her?"

"Illness, accidents. The files say the children died of their own accord."

"Don't they get suspicious? I mean, about all the children who go missing?"

"She lies. She keeps some of them alive through their records. Then says they are ill or indisposed when the inspector comes."

"They believe her? They don't ask to see the children?" Ishi inquired, astonished.

"They do not care. They are just checking off boxes to meet the requirements of the law, Ishi. They are doing what it takes to keep the money flowing in their direction."

Ishi's head was spinning. Did nobody care? He walked into the room and sat on his bed, his mind reeling with the knowledge. They were "discards", only kept alive because they were children. He shook his head in disbelief.

"Do they care about children? I mean, the world out there? Is that why we are here?"

Oslo didn't answer and Ishi began to understand. They were broken, but they were children. Ms. Virginia was simply hiding a dirty secret the world didn't want to acknowledge. Did his parents not want him, then? They sold him away? Did the powers that be keep them alive only because they were children and it appeased their guilt? Why bother educating them?

Oslo reached out and put his fingered hand on Ishi's shoulder, knowing the boy was hurting. Ishi peered up at the robot and began to weep.

Oslo sat next to him and drew the boy to his metal chest. "You must not let the world win."

Ishi had all but given up hope. They didn't have a value, they were something to be locked away and forgotten. He stared at his twisted leg and more than ever wished he could chop it off and grow a new one. Not because of his feelings on it, though it did slow him down at times.

However, now he felt like it was a mark of shame.

He wiped his nose and sat back, taking a shuddering breath. "Why don't they just kill us when we are babies, why send us here and pay Ms. Virginia to teach us? To keep us alive?"

"Humans are strange in their motivations. They do it so they can believe they are not monsters," Oslo replied.

"They *are* monsters! We're people, just like them!" Ishi yelled, knowing if he was heard he might also be taken to the hole. "We deserve to be treated with dignity."

"Fools do not know dignity."

Ishi thought about those words. Whoever was in charge wasn't paying for them to be there. That probably came from all the people who wanted to hide these discards away. Out of sight, out of mind. Rage filled him as he considered the value of his life. Zero. He was nothing.

Oslo rose and walked toward the door, stopping to face Ishi. "I am scrap, that is what Ms. Virginia says. You are a discard. We can believe that, or we can decide it is not true."

"Then what?"

Oslo waved his hand in the air. "Then we fight."

He scooted out the door, leaving Ishi alone with his thoughts. Fight? How? One Moscow could destroy them all and Ms. Virginia had an army of Moscows. Ishi thought about the night the power went out and the robots were rendered useless.

The Raiders. They'd come to the island and knocked the power grid out. Ishi didn't know why they came or if they, too, were heartless beings, but they'd come and knew how to dismantle the system. Maybe if he could get off the island and find them, he could seek their assistance.

Perhaps they were there to hurt the children. Or kidnap them to get their stipend, but Ishi didn't think so. In his heart, he felt they were his only hope. If he stayed, both he and Darius would be dead.

Leaving the island was his only chance at survival and saving the children of the island. However, he'd spent his most of his life there and had no idea how to get off the island or where to go.

He'd seen maps of the world in their studies, but he didn't know where the island was situated in comparison to the other landmasses. Nor did he have a boat. Ms. Virginia had made it very hard to leave the prison she'd created for them. Ishi knew if he didn't act fast, Dari would disappear. He couldn't let that happen.

As he lay in his bed, he thought about the island, the seasons, the way the wind blew, and the inspector. The inspector came every month. He didn't seem like he'd traveled far and came and went on the same day. So, he was able to make it to the island, do his inspection, and go home all within about twenty-four hours. The mainland couldn't be too far.

Ishi remembered the supply boat was coming the day after next. They grew much of their own food, but once a week a boat would drop off anything they couldn't make. Mostly stuff for Ms. Virginia, like her delicacies and items she wanted for herself. Her space was filled with things the children were never allowed to enjoy and she'd not go without those special items. Gourmet foods, silk sheets, trinkets from far-off lands. Ishi knew the only way off the island was to hijack the boat when it came. To sneak on and drive it away from the island while they were distracted.

First, he needed to save Darius.

# Chapter Seven

After Moscow made his rounds, Ishi slipped out of bed and crept along the wall toward the door. Darius hadn't returned to the room and Ishi knew his time was limited.

The children always went missing at night, never during the day. He wasn't sure what happened to them, but he figured starting at Ms. Virginia's room was the best option. He didn't tell Oslo his plan, as he didn't want the robot to be punished for his transgressions.

Peering out into the hall, Ishi saw it was clear and inched along, trying to stay in the shadows. None of the other boys followed him and he was glad for that. It was going to be hard enough to get himself to Ms. Virginia's room unseen, a gaggle of boys would only make it obvious.

A sound caught his attention and he ducked into a dark corner, seeing Moscow carrying a tray of utensils from the medical room. Medical room... not like they were ever treated for ailments, but the inspector always asked to see it. Ishi pondered why he never cared about the missing children. Moscow rounded the bend to Ms. Virginia's hallway and Ishi tiptoed to trail him.

Once Moscow got to Ms. Virginia's room, he set the tray down outside the door and knocked. An angry voice told him to enter and he did as he was told. The door closed partially behind the robot, a sliver of light coming out into the hall. Ishi could hear crying and snuck up to the door, pressing an eye to the slit. He could see the shadow of Ms. Virginia moving around and heard whimpering.

Darius.

Ishi almost bumped the tray and stared down at it. His heart began to race when he realized what he was looking at. Surgical tools. Scalpels, clamps, something that looked like it was meant to pull things out of the body. They were going to use those on Darius! Without thinking, Ishi picked up the tray and hid it in a nearby closet. Moscow came to the door and Ishi ran to hide.

The robot came to where he'd set the tray and stared down at the empty space with what could be deemed as close to confusion as a robot could express. He spun and glanced around the hall, not sure where his errant tray of tools went.

"Moscow!" A shrill yell came from inside Ms. Virginia's room. "Bring me those tools, now!"

Moscow stood unmoving, unsure how to proceed. Ms. Virginia stormed into the hall and glared at him. He pointed to where the tools had been and simply said, "Gone."

Ms. Virginia turned bright red and slapped him, though from the sound of her soft hand hitting metal, it hurt her more than him. She grabbed him by the arm and dragged him back to the medical office, convinced the robot had forgotten to bring the tray.

"Stupid hunk of garbage. I'll show you where the tools are. I mean, if I wasn't here..." her voice trailed off as they disappeared down the hall.

Ishi jumped into action and ran into Ms. Virginia's room. Darius was bruised and bleeding, tied to a chair. Ishi scanned the room and saw a pair of scissors on the desk. He quickly cut through the bindings, talking to Dari to let him know he was there.

"We need to get you out of here! I think they're going to hurt you."

Dari's head lifted and wobbled, his eyes blank as he listened to Ishi. "They did hurt me. She said they are going to sell my body parts."

Ishi shuddered. Was that where the other children went? They were killed and dismembered for body parts? How was she getting away with that? Ishi tried to figure out what was happening, but he was running out of time. He needed to get Darius somewhere safe before they came back for him. Once they saw Dari was gone, they'd tear the place apart, searching for him.

He lifted the slight boy and led him to the door, peeking out to see if Ms. Virginia was coming back. She wasn't, but he could hear her hollering and carrying on from the other hall. He darted out, pulling Dari along, not sure where to go next. Just as he realized he'd boxed them in with no escape, a door near him flung open. He stifled a scream, sure they were done for when a little bit of light reflected off metal.

Oslo.

A hand reached out and tugged them into the dark space. Ishi didn't know if Oslo would help or turn them in. His question was answered at that moment.

"I will take Dari, I have a hiding place. You go back to your bed. They are going to search once they realize he is gone," Oslo ordered.

"I can't. I'd have to go by them to get back," Ishi explained.

"There are secret passages. Behind us is a grate, it leads to a tunnel behind the walls. Follow it until you get to the eleventh vent and push it open. This will be the boys' room. Eleven."

Ishi was shocked. He stared at Oslo, who waved his hand toward the grate. Ishi hustled toward it and yanked the grate off. He climbed in and was surprised to see Oslo following him. Oslo pushed Dari into the space and motioned for Ishi to move. The robot closed the grate behind them and they began to crawl through the tunnel. About halfway down, Oslo stopped at another vent. Ishi turned and frowned.

"Where are you going?"

Oslo pushed the vent grate open. "I have a place to hide. It is not here, we need to go through the woods to a bunker."

A bunker? Ishi stared blankly. There was a lot more to Oslo than he'd suspected. "Oslo, I need to get off the island, to go find help. Me and Darius. Can you help?"

Oslo shook his head as he guided Dari through the vent. "Not now. Soon."

"I don't have much time," Ishi whispered.

Oslo met his eyes and nodded. "I know. Trust me."

The robot and Dari disappeared into the blackness and Ishi could hear Ms. Virginia screaming from the vents. They'd discovered Darius was gone and were about to wake all the children. He needed to move! He shuffled through the tunnel, losing track of the number of vents. Finally, he came to one he thought went to the boys' room and shoved with all his might. The effort caused him to spill out onto the floor with a thud. Jumping up, he slammed the grate shut and gazed around. He was in the boys' room and he could hear Moscow coming down the hall.

Despite his leg hindering him without his cane, he moved as fast as he could across the room to his bed, landing in it just as the lights flooded on and the shadow of Moscow darkened the door. Ishi tried to steady his breathing and make it look like he'd been startled awake like the other boys.

Moscow tore through the room, flipping beds and flinging any children in his way. Ms. Virginia came to the door and glared at them like a hawk, trying to get a read on if any of them knew what happened to Darius. Her eyes landed on Ishi. She stormed across the room, snatching him up by his shirt.

"What do you know?" she bellowed, shaking him violently like a ragdoll.

Ishi trembled, sure he'd been caught when one of the other boys spoke up. "Ms. Virginia, Ishi has been here sleeping."

She whipped around and slapped the small boy. "Who asked you?"

The boy didn't answer but her attention had been diverted. She stomped around the room almost without focus, then left. Ishi met the boy's eyes and nodded.

"Thank you, Timmy."

The boy smiled and sat back on the edge of his bed. No matter what, the children knew they only had each other. Timmy's story was much like the rest of them. He had a heart condition, a hole in his heart. He wasn't able to do manual labor, but he was bright and Ms. Virginia had him work on fixing the computers that ran the different systems. She wasn't willing to punish him too severely for that reason. Ishi thought about it and considered Timmy might be one he needed to take with him.

After a couple of hours and the place had been ransacked, the lights cut off. They didn't find Darius and the other children were left to clean up their space in the dark. It felt like they'd just gone back to sleep when the lights cut on again and they were directed to their daily stations. Ishi headed for the kitchen, feeling like all eyes were on him.

Ms. Virginia was waiting in the kitchen with another boy, who was around eleven years old. She shoved the boy toward Ishi and snarked, "Train him to do your job. You have til the end of the week."

Ishi knew this meant they were preparing to get rid of him. He didn't have a choice and began showing the boy how to prep the meager and rotten food, explaining how important it was to remove certain parts and cook everything else until it was almost mush to make sure they didn't get sick. Or *as* sick. The boy listened but kept glancing at the door.

"Don't worry, she leaves me alone when I'm in here. I actually kinda like it because I can think and cook."

The boy nodded and focused on the potato he was chopping. His fingers were fused together on each hand, so he had to work around the knife by pinching it like a claw. Ishi wanted to step in and help but knew the boy needed to learn to do it his way, so he could keep working in the kitchen.

By the time the food was done, the boy had caught on... enough. While Ishi was glad, he also knew it was one more string to his life that was being cut. He helped the boy carry the food to the cafeteria and noticed Ms. Virginia standing in the hall with a smirk on her face. He put his head down, focusing on serving the meal.

Later that day, Ishi saw Oslo down the hall and wanted to ask him about Darius, but he knew they needed to make it seem like nothing had happened. Oslo came toward him, pushing a cart of laundry. Ishi went to step aside when Oslo beelined for him, knocking Ishi down.

Ishi hit his head on the wall and stared up at Oslo in confusion. The robot shook his head angrily and grumbled, "Disrespectful child! Gather this laundry up!"

Ishi slid over and began scooping laundry back into the bin. Oslo seemed to be ignoring him until he turned and slipped something into Ishi's waistband.

The robot rose and pointed to the bathrooms. "Go clean yourself up! Dirty and clumsy!"

Ishi got to his feet and stumbled to the bathroom, making sure the item in his waistband stayed put. He went into a stall and pulled it out, his heart thumping in his chest.

It was a map!

# Chapter Eight

K nowing his time was running out, Ishi gazed at the map, trying to understand what he was looking at. It was of the island, however, much of what he saw on the paper was of areas the children weren't allowed to go. Ms. Virginia had very strict rules about where they were permitted to be. This map showed a whole island, a dock, and buildings he'd never been to. Ishi was intrigued and folded the map back into his waistband.

What caught his attention the most was an area marked with a black circle. Clearly written in by Oslo. Ishi assumed Oslo was letting him know where he'd taken Darius. Ishi thought about how bad it would be if the map ended up in the wrong hands and considered flushing it. With his luck, it would back up the toilet, so he left it pressed between the fabric of his waistband and his skin.

As he departed the bathroom, he could hear Ms. Virginia talking down another hall and distinctly heard her say his name and the word, "tonight." His birthday wasn't for a few more days but it seemed she intended to get rid of him before then. She must've suspected his involvement in Dari's disappearance. He paused and weighed his options. He could wait until nightfall and slip out then. However, he wasn't sure when they'd come for him. He couldn't risk it.

Remembering the tunnel system, Ishi headed for the nearest grate and unscrewed the hardware holding it on. Once he had it loose, he climbed in and yanked the grate shut behind him. They'd notice him missing almost right away, but hopefully, they wouldn't know where to look for him. He pressed back against the interior wall and waited. Children passed him, never knowing he was in there.

He wondered who knew about the tunnels and assumed Ms. Virginia and the other robots didn't, as they never looked for Darius there.

Within fifteen minutes, he knew they'd discovered he was missing from the alarms going off. He squeezed himself as far back as he could, watching the children and robots running down the hall in search of him. It fell silent, then he heard the distinct shifting of Ms. Virginia's large frame coming slowly down the hall. It was as if she was aware of exactly where he was hiding. She even stopped outside the grate and stood, her raspy breath creating anxiety in Ishi.

"Boy, you can't hide from me. I'll find you. This is an island, there is no escape," she whispered as if she was speaking directly to him.

Ishi moved away, hoping she wouldn't think to peer in the grate. If she did, he'd be caught. She leaned against the wall and began humming to herself. Like cat and mouse.

Did she know he was in there?

Right about the time Ishi was sure he was trapped, he heard metal feet coming down the hall. Ms Virginia stepped forward away from the grate, causing light to stream in without her blocking it.

"What do you want?" she growled.

"Ms. Virginia, we think we found him," came Oslo's voice. "We discovered his pack out by the gardens."

Ishi held his breath. He hadn't been out to the gardens and certainly hadn't taken his pack there. They weren't allowed to carry bags or personal items with them, so someone had taken his pack from his footlocker and planted it out by the garden. Planted it. The connection almost made Ishi laugh but he was too smart to let it escape. Ms. Virginia huffed and followed the rickety robot out to the gardens.

Ishi knew Oslo was creating a diversion so he could escape and there was no going back. He needed to go to the place marked with the black circle on the map. He hoped Dari would be there and they could flee together.

As soon as the coast was clear, Ishi made his way down the tunnel, checking each grate he passed. When he came to the one that went to the laundry room, he prepared his escape. Clothes were washed but had to be hung out to dry on sunny days, so there was a door off of the washroom. That led to the meadow that bordered the forest. He would be seen in the field since there were no trees but needed to risk it. If he moved fast enough, he could get to the wood line within minutes and from there could use the map to find his way.

Ishi pushed open the grate and peered around. He was alone. He darted to the door and ran out without thinking. As soon as his feet hit the ground outside, he smashed into something, knocking him back on his behind. Convinced he was caught, he began to stammer out an excuse.

"I saw Dari and went after him," he muttered.

"No you didn't," a familiar voice replied.

Ishi stared up into the face of Jai as she rebalanced the load of laundry on her hip she was bringing in. He wasn't sure what he could say to her, so rose and helped her scoop up the fallen sheets. "Sorry."

"What are you doing out here? I heard they were looking for you," Jai asked, sizing him up.

"Don't tell anyone. They're going to kill me. They tried to kill Darius, but he escaped," Ishi explained, leaving Oslo and the details out of it.

Jai tipped her head, glancing past him. "Well, you'd better go, then."

Ishi paused, not convinced she wouldn't call him out and get him in trouble. "Thanks, Jai."

She set down the basket and smoothed her tattered dress. "I'm going with you."

"No!" Ishi cried. He couldn't risk taking the skinny girl with him. She'd slow him down. She'd be another missing child and they'd scour the island looking for them. He backed away, planning to make a run for the woods when she narrowed her eyes at him.

"I'm going with you and that's final. I hate it here. I need to go back home and make things right."

Make things right? Did this girl not understand what she was up against? Ishi knew he couldn't stop her if she wanted to follow him. If he refused, she could make things very hard for him. She was the only one who'd seen him and there weren't enough places to hide. He took a deep breath and blew it out, allowing the frustration to dissipate.

"If you come, you need to listen to me on everything. I have a plan, but can't tell you in case you get caught and they torture you."

"Torture me?" Jai asked, fear lacing her words.

"What do you think happens to the children who go missing here? What do you think they do to them?" Ishi questioned, trying to get her to understand the gravity of the situation.

Jai visibly gulped and nodded. "I'll listen."

Ishi scanned around, considering the best escape route when Jai put her hand on his arm. "Follow me."

She picked up the laundry basket and began walking between rows of sheets. Ishi trailed behind her, his eyes darting every which way, expecting Moscow or Ms. Virginia to pop out from behind the sun-bleached bedding.

When they got to the edge of the last row, Jai set down her basket and cocked her head. "On three. Ready? One, two, three!"

She bolted out of the row of laundry for the woods. Ishi's mouth hung open, realizing there was no way back now. He ran as fast as he could after her, his leg causing him grief and slowing him down. When they got to the tree line, he collapsed, ignoring the throbbing in his thigh. He vigorously rubbed the leg, knowing he could only pause for a moment. He needed to keep moving.

"What happened to your leg? I mean, before?" Jai asked, catching her breath.

Ishi shrugged. "Ms. Virginia said I was injured as a child, but I don't remember any of it. She said I was only a little over a year old."

"Oh. So, that's why you were sent here?"

"I guess so. I don't trust anything anymore," Ishi replied and pulled himself up with a tree branch. His cane was long gone and he'd need to make do with what he could find. He tugged out the map and peered at it. He didn't know the other areas but was able to track a trail from the laundry room to where the black circle was.

"This way."

"Where are we going? Where did you get that map? What are we going to do?" Jai asked, her questions running together like one long sentence.

"I'm going to find Dari, and find a way off this island."

"How?"

"There's a boat that comes every week. It's due by tomorrow morning. As soon as they get off, I'm jumping on and taking it."

"You know how to drive a boat?" Jai asked incredulously.

"Uh, no."

"Do you have keys?"

Also no. Ishi fell silent, considering the holes in his plan. "I'll figure it out."

Jai walked behind him, her head bent in thought. "If you do get it started, do you know where to go?"

Ishi was getting tired of all her questions but knew she was right... to a degree. "I got this far, didn't I?" he snapped at her.

Jai picked up a pine cone, twirling it in her fingers. "Did you, though?"

This stopped Ishi in his tracks.

Technically, Oslo got him to the laundry room and Jai got him to the forest. He sighed and shook his head. "I guess not."

Jai smiled and tossed the pine cone. "Don't worry, you have me now!"

Ishi couldn't help but chuckle at the small girl. He reached back his hand and was relieved when she took it. Even if he didn't want company, he had it now and needed all the help he could get. They wandered in silence, Ishi glancing at the map now and then to make sure they stayed on track.

After about an hour, he was sure he'd gotten them lost and stopped to assess where they were. He held the map up and frowned. "I don't think we are where we are supposed to be. Nothing is here."

Jai gazed over his shoulder and touched the black circle on the map, then pointed off into the woods. "So, that's not it?"

Ishi stared at where she was pointing when he spied some sort of structure. A boat house! He looked at the map and in fact, the circle seemed to be around the boat house. He squeezed Jai's hand and they crept through the woods until they were on the edge of the clearing for the boat house. It seemed abandoned.

They went closer and peered in the grimy windows. The space was empty and in disrepair. Before he could stop her, Jai pushed open the door.

"Hello? Anyone in here?" she called.

Ishi felt his heart hit the floor. Not only was Darius not in there, Jai was making it obvious they were there. He pulled her inside and slammed the door shut, glaring at her. "Shhh. You'll give us away."

Jai seemed unperturbed and began checking out the space. Ishi was convinced they'd hit a dead end and rotated the map in his hands. "I must've read it wrong."

Jai wasn't listening and stared out the window, her eyes growing wide. "They're coming! I can see Moscow in the woods. What do we do now?"

Ishi scooted over beside her and could see motion in the foliage. They had nowhere to go, no way out. He peered around the space, searching for a place to hide when a door in the floor flung open. Oslo's head peeked out.

"You made it. Come on, we are hiding down here!"

# Chapter Nine

The stairs going down were rickety and Ishi wondered how Oslo managed them. As soon as they were at the bottom, Oslo pulled the covering shut and motioned to move down an enclosed, dimly lit tunnel that opened into a cave-like room. Ishi stared around, perplexed by the space. He turned to Oslo in question.

"Where did this come from?" he whispered.

Oslo tipped his head. "I am not sure."

"Not sure? How did you find it, then?" Ishi asked in confusion.

Oslo seemed uncomfortable and pushed Ishi gently into the large room. Ishi was immediately distracted from his thoughts when he saw Darius and ran over to him, scooping the boy up in his arms. "Dari!"

"Ishi!" the boy cried back, clinging to his friend.

Jai moved in behind and touched Dari on the shoulder. "Hey, Darius."

"Jai! Is anyone else here with you?" Dari asked.

"Just me, Jai, and Oslo," Ishi replied, relieved to see his young friend again.

"And Timmy," Oslo added, surprising both Jai and Ishi, who glanced around the dark space to see the boy.

Timmy stepped out of the shadows, grinning. "Hi."

Ishi was delighted but unclear as to why Timmy was there and faced Oslo. "Was he...?"

He didn't have to finish. Oslo nodded. "When they could not find Darius, they had to meet their order quota, so they went for Timmy. I overheard and brought him here."

Their order quota? Ishi felt his blood run cold and shivered. "I see. So, when they don't find Timmy?"

Oslo turned away, unable to meet Ishi's eyes. "I cannot stop them. We need help."

"Who will help us?" Jai asked, her voice sounding defeated and cynical.

Ishi watched Oslo and could tell the robot knew something he didn't. "Oslo?"

Oslo moved past them into the space and motioned for them to sit down. The group of children followed and filled in around him. Oslo stared off, doing something Ishi had never seen the robots do. He seemed to be considering. Not regurgitating information, rather mulling it over in his mind.

Finally, Oslo spoke. "What I am about to tell you can go nowhere. It is a secret I have carried for a long, long time. Did you know I was here before Ms. Virginia?"

That shocked the children and they audibly gasped. Ishi rubbed his forehead, attempting to understand. "How did you get here?"

"There were people on the island before the others came. Ms. Virginia was granted the island to run a children's camp. The people that were here before were indigenous. Do you know what that means?" Oslo asked.

"They were from here originally," Jai answered.

"Yes. This was their home. Then, the government decided they needed it more and made the people leave."

"Leave? Where did they go? What if they didn't want to go?" Ishi questioned.

Oslo shook his head. "If they did not go, they were imprisoned or killed. If they did go, I do not know where specifically. They try to stay on the move to not get caught."

A question still nagged at Ishi. "So, if they were indigenous, how did you get here?"

"These people, they are very smart. More advanced than the rest of society. They were the first ones to build robots here. They obtained parts from different areas by traveling and brought them back here to build robots. They created me."

"Oooh," Darius whispered in awe. "That's amazing. Why did they build you?"

"They believed robots could help stop what was happening in the world. Assist them in fighting against what they saw as ultimate destruction."

"Why didn't they take you with them?" Ishi asked. "That seems mean to leave you behind."

"On the contrary. My job is here, my purpose is with you," Oslo explained.

"With us? How could they have known we'd be brought here?" Jai inquired.

"They did not know about you all per se, but they knew the island was to be used as some sort of prison camp."

"Prison? What does that mean?" Timmy asked.

"A prison is a place where they lock up people they see as a threat," Oslo answered.

"How are we a threat?" Ishi replied, aghast. How could children hurt anyone?

"Ah, yes. You are not a threat in a way you could harm them, rather your presence makes them uncomfortable. They do not want to see you," Oslo said.

The room fell silent as each of them considered what that meant. Ishi felt hot tears spring to his eyes and he pushed them back. Now, more than ever, he felt unwanted and discarded. He met Oslo's eyes. "So, why are you here? To protect us?"

Oslo watched him, his eyes calculating. "Not exactly. My job is to observe and report."

"What does that mean?" Darius chimed in.

"I am to record whatever I see happening and tell the people who left me here. They are always aware. They tried to overtake the island but have been unsuccessful so far."

"If they did, would they hurt us?" Timmy asked.

"No. They do not harm anyone unless they are attacked. They could just kill Ms. Virginia, but are attempting to take back their land without harm if possible."

"Ms. Virginia should be killed," Jai muttered under her breath.

Oslo reached out and placed his pincher hand gently on her shoulder. "You have every right to be angry, however, you do not want to become like the people that put you here."

Jai stood up, brushing off his arm. "Maybe I do! Children go missing. They're killing children! Give me one good reason why I shouldn't stab a knife into Ms. Virginia's heart?"

Oslo waited a moment, glancing between all the children. "She is only one, they are a million. You would not stop them."

"But we'd stop her," Ishi said.

"True, but when the inspectors came out and found her dead, then what?" Oslo countered.

Ishi thought about how that would play out and imagined they'd kill all the children out of revenge. He stared between his friends and knew they needed to find another way. They could take the boat to the mainland and see if they could report her, maybe get her arrested. If nothing else, maybe they could get the children off the island. Back to his original plan of stealing the boat.

"Tomorrow, I'll wait until the supplies are being unloaded, then sneak on board the boat. Once they leave to transport the supplies up to the house, I'll take it to the mainland."

"I want to go," Dari insisted.

The other two children agreed and Ishi understood there was no way around it. He turned to Oslo. "Will you come with us? Have you ever been?"

Oslo shook his head. "I have not. I was built here and have never left. But I will go with you. It would be good if I was there in case you come across the people of this island. The Maboni."

"Maboni?" Timmy asked.

"That is what they call themselves. It is their ancestral name, though they go by another, as well. They know about you children and are trying to get to you."

"They do? Why?" Ishi questioned.

"They understand your plight. They are aware what it is like to be driven from their homes and be abandoned by those they trusted. You can count on them," Oslo explained.

Ishi's head began to throb and he lay down on the cool dirt floor. Oslo rose and went to the opening leading to the tunnel. "I must go check on things. To make sure no one is around. Get some rest and we will talk more later. There is food and blankets in the box by the wall over there. Eat and rest. We have a big day tomorrow."

The children rifled through the box, happy to find unrotten food to eat. Mostly bread and a little cheese, but it was more and better food than they'd had since being on the island. Once they ate and drank clean water, they spread the blankets out and rested together on the floor. Dari and Timmy dozed off, however, Ishi's brain was going a mile a minute. He was nervous about stealing the boat, but he knew there was no other way. He felt his eyes get heavy when Jai spoke.

"People on the mainland... well, they're different," she whispered.

"Different how?" Ishi asked.

"Things there, they are like, um, really clean. But not in a good way. What they decide is dirty gets thrown away."

Ishi thought about that but didn't understand.

What did she mean by dirty? Everything on the island was used until it pretty much disintegrated or was recycled into something else. Even their clothes were worn until the threads simply gave way. Dirt could be washed, broken could be fixed... sometimes.

"I don't understand."

Jai sighed, not out of frustration, out of trying to find the words. "Like us. They consider us dirty."

"Oh." Ishi still didn't comprehend, but he understood what it felt like to be unwanted.

Jai rolled over and went to sleep, leaving Ishi alone with his thoughts. Hijacking the boat was only the first challenge. Making it to the mainland and getting help was a whole other problem. Especially if they were considered dirty.

He heard Oslo come back and take a station near the children. Ishi sat up to let Oslo know he was still awake. The robot seemed tired in a way only he could.

"Oslo? Are we safe?"

"For now. We cannot hide here for long. They have ways of finding children. We will be fine until tomorrow, but we need to get on that boat and get off the island."

"I'm scared."

"I know. It is only natural to be scared, however, leaving is better than staying. Besides, there are people who want to help."

"The Maboni?" Ishi asked, running the name across his tongue.

"Yes, the Maboni and other tribes like them," Oslo agreed.

"There are more?"

"All around the world, people like them were driven from their lands. They are a peaceful people, but will fight for what is rightfully theirs."

"Why would they want to help us, then? Aren't we on their land?"

"You are, but like them, it was not your choice. They understand you have been driven from your home, as well. Ishi, now you must rest. Tomorrow will be a long and harrowing day. You need your strength."

Ishi yawned and laid back down. A thought crossed his mind and he turned to Oslo. "You said they are called by another name? The Maboni?"

"Yes, they are. They are also known as Raiders."

# Chapter Ten

"T he Raiders?" Ishi cried out. "I thought they were attacking us?"

"Not attacking you," Oslo answered. "They were attacking the compound. They were trying to reclaim the island, to get rid of Ms. Virginia."

Ishi thought about that. If they got rid of Ms. Virginia, what would happen to all of the children? "Where would we go?"

"Ishi, they have no issue with you. You are like them."

"Would they keep us?"

Oslo shifted, his metal joints creaking. "I do not know. They would not hurt you, I know that."

"Making us leave our home would hurt us," Ishi whispered.

"Well, that is true. From what I understand, they would help you, but I am unsure what that means, exactly. I do know they were trying to save you children last time."

"I see." Ishi wasn't sure he did but Oslo seemed fine with it. He trusted Oslo, as much as one can trust a robot. Ishi drew his legs to his chest and closed his eyes. "I'm tired."

Oslo nodded, his eyes dimming. "Get some sleep. I need to go up to the boat house to power up and check on things. I will not be far and you are safe down here. Ishi?"

"Yes?"

"It will be okay."

"How can you know that?"

Oslo rose and moved toward the tunnel. "Because it has not been for so long and it is time for things to change."

He slipped down the tunnel and Ishi dozed off. He dreamed of walking through the woods, tripping over parts of disassembled robots. It was dark and he couldn't find his way, calling out for Oslo. All of a sudden, something grabbed his foot and he jerked away, staring down at his captor. A robot arm flailed around on the ground, no longer attached to its owner. As Ishi peered closer, he gasped. It was Oslo's arm.

Frantic, he searched around the area for the rest of his friend, but Oslo was nowhere to be found. Ishi heard a baby crying and stumbled toward the sound. Around the back of a large oak tree, he found a baby shoe and a blanket. Frowning, he picked it up and looked at the fabric. A name was stitched into the blue fabric and he ran his fingers over it. *Ishmael.*

Ishmael? Was that a name? He liked the way it sounded if he was saying it right as he whispered it over and over. For some reason, it felt like home. Clinging to the soft knitted fabric, Ishi wandered further into the woods, still hearing the baby crying. As he rounded another tree, he saw a small, dark-haired boy with deep golden skin like his own. The boy was trapped under a fallen tree. Ishi came up to the boy and crouched down, easing the branches and debris off the child. The boy turned his large brown eyes to Ishi, tears spilling out of the corners. He couldn't have been older than about two years old. If even.

"What's your name?" Ishi asked the boy.

"I Ishmael," the boy whispered, his baby words chubby and full.

"Ishmael. I am Ishi."

The boy reached out for Ishi, so he scooped the toddler into his arms and carried him on his hip. The boy rested his head on Ishi's shoulder and muttered, "Sleepy."

"Shhh, rest on my arm, I'll carry you," Ishi said, his voice soothing.

He heard a woman calling for the boy through the forest and headed in the direction of her voice. However, as he came into view of the woman, the boy in his arms disappeared and Ishi stood in the trees, his brow knitted. The boy was gone. The woman spied him and flung her arms out wide.

"Ishmael! I have been looking for you everywhere. You shouldn't wander away, child."

Ishi rotated to look around him but the boy was nowhere to be seen. Why did the woman think she saw him? She ran over and embraced Ishi, rubbing his back. Ishi was confused but liked the way she felt so he stood in place, allowing himself to feel nurtured for the first time he could remember. She stepped back, cupping his chin in her hand.

"I was worried about you. You need to stay close."

Ishi nodded and trailed behind her when she moved deep into the woods. She seemed to know where she was going and he didn't want to be far from her. Maybe the boy would show back up if they stayed together.

Ishi paused and spoke. "Who are you?"

The woman turned with a smirk. "Ishmael, don't be silly. I'm your mother."

Ishi thought that made sense, after all, she was searching for the boy. Ishmael. He wasn't sure why she kept calling him by the boy's name. Unless it wasn't his name. Maybe a term of endearment. However, she said she was his mother and he was much older than the boy.

The woman kept walking and in an instant was gone, as if the trees absorbed her. Ishi didn't want her to go and cried out, "Lady? Ma'am? Mother?"

He was greeted by silence. He ran ahead, stopping short when he saw red eyes watching him through the trees. Robot eyes. Panic filled him and he went to turn back when a huge hole opened in front of him and he fell.

With a jerk, Ishi woke up, a scream caught in his throat. He was in the room under the boat house and the other children were still sleeping. Oslo was nowhere to be seen, so Ishi went over and climbed next to Timmy. The boy turned and placed his hand on Ishi's chest. Ishi smiled, even though he felt like crying. The woman had been so real. She'd felt like everything he thought a mother would feel like. It was only a dream, though.

A little while later, Oslo came in and settled with his back against the dirt wall. Ishi watched him, still trying to make out the details of the dream. It made him sad Oslo was dismembered in the dream. Oslo saw him staring and increased the light in his eyes.

"Ishi, have you slept?"

"A little. I had a strange dream. You were... I guess, hurt in the dream," Ishi admitted.

"Oh? Well, I am fine. All charged up."

"How long does that last?"

Oslo tapped his claw fingers together. "Seven days, as long as I do not use my power externally."

"How do you do that?"

"I can power things at times. If needed," Oslo explained and dimmed his eyes.

"Oslo, how long will it take to get to the mainland on the boat?"

"It depends on where we go. The closest is a few hours. However, I do not think we should go there."

"Why" Ishi asked.

"It is very monitored. We will not get close without them spying us. I think we should go up the coast to a more remote area."

"I see. Will we be in danger?"

"I imagine so. You were sent here for a reason, I doubt they will want you showing back up," Oslo answered.

"Oh. I suppose you're right. Do you know... I mean, how will we find the Raiders?"

"They will find us. I am hoping we find them before we arrive on the mainland. Otherwise, we will be outnumbered and lost."

"Lost?"

"I am not familiar with that world. I know maps, but without a guide, we run the risk of getting disoriented or caught," Oslo replied.

"If we get caught, what will happen?" Ishi asked, suddenly doubting their plan. What was the saying Ms. Virginia always spouted at them?

*Better than the devil you know than the devil you don't.*

That was it. He never really understood, but now he did. They were running from Ms. Virginia, however, they might be heading right for the mouth of hell. He shuddered at the thought and wondered if they could safely go back.

No, of course, they couldn't. Ms. Virginia would kill all of them. The only way out was to keep moving. They made the choice, now they had to follow through with it. Ishi sensed a calm come over him. He needed to keep the other three children safe. Oslo would be there, too. He glanced at Oslo.

"Oslo, why are you helping us?"

Oslo turned his large, metallic eyes to Ishi and cocked his head. "You are my family."

This made Ishi want to cry. Oslo was right. The other robots were Ms. Virginia's, however, Oslo had always been for the children. Watching out for them, protecting them, assisting them.

"I love you, Oslo," he whispered.

Oslo's face showed a form of emotion Ishi had never seen. The robots rarely had expressions that seemed human, yet Oslo seemed to be expressing care. Oslo bobbed his head. "I love you too, Ishi."

"Do you know what love is?"

"Of course. I am not like the other robots. I was created out of love, I was loved. I understand the way a mother loves a child."

This reminded Ishi of his dream and seeing Oslo's arm. He thought of the boy and the woman. "Oslo, have you heard the name Ishmael before?"

Oslo's head snapped toward Ishi, his eyes burning bright. "Where did you hear that name?"

"I-I had a dream and there was a little boy named Ishmael in it. His mother was looking for him."

Oslo listened, his eyes flickering. He shook his head. "Ishi, I have seen Ms. Virginia's files. Whenever I cleaned in there, I would peek at her records. I know who Ishmael is."

"Really?" Ishi bolted up, his eyes wide. "Who?"

"You, Ishi. You are Ishmael."

# Chapter Eleven

*I* *shmael.* Ishi let the name settle in his mind, liking the new familiarity. He wasn't just Ishi. He was Ishmael.

Did that make the woman in his dream his mother? She seemed to think so. He let the warmth of the thought send tingles down his spine.

His mother.

Oslo went on to tell him how he'd come to the island, according to his records. He'd been crushed by a tree as a young child. Like the boy in the dream. There was no other information except after he'd been crushed, Ishi was taken to the hospital. His parents couldn't afford to pay the bill, so he'd been taken away from them. They were charged with failure to provide care and he'd been absorbed into the system. His father was imprisoned. Then it skipped to him being assigned to Ms. Virginia and his life on the island.

*Palashtu.* That was scribbled on the records but Ishi didn't know what it meant. Oslo told him there was once an area called Palashtu, but that its people had been driven from their land, forcing them to be nomadic. Homeless of sorts. Ishi didn't know if those were his people, but it sounded like they were much like the other indigenous people Oslo spoke of. The Raiders.

Maybe his family was still out there searching for him. If he could find them, he could go home. If he *had* a home. The idea created a spark in his chest. Desire. For the first time since he could remember, he had something to hope for.

Ishi wasn't sure when he dozed off, but he didn't dream again. He slept heavily, like after a long illness. Sunlight woke him and he could hear Darius and Timmy whispering between themselves. Jai was still sleeping and Ishi didn't want to disturb her. It was going to be a stressful day and if they were successful stealing the boat, it would be their last time on the island for a while.

Oslo was nowhere to be seen but a small bucket was by the door. Ishi peered in and was delighted to see bread and berries. Oslo must have taken the bread from Ms. Virginia as it was much too fresh to be from the children's kitchen. The berries were still warm from being picked and Ishi wondered how Oslo managed that with his misshapen hands.

Ishi divided the food four ways and doled it out to the other children, leaving his aside to make sure they got enough. Once the boys had eaten, he nibbled on his, wanting to devour it but also wanting to make it last since he didn't know when they'd eat again. Jai woke and ate her food, her face drawn into a frown.

Ishi went and sat beside her, staring at the food. "Is it not good?"

She shook her head. "No, it's fine. I just don't know if I'm ready for today. To go back."

"To the mainland?" Ishi questioned.

"Yes. Things are hard here, but better than my life there. There, I was always afraid and hungry."

Ishi thought about what she'd told him about being locked away and starved, then shuddered. At least on the island, they had three meals. Not great meals, but still it was some food. He put his arm over her shoulder when he noticed tears trickling down her cheeks. He had no words to make it better and figured nothing would make a difference, anyway. He hugged her and they sat eating in silence.

When Oslo returned, the children were antsy and ready to make a plan. Oslo came in and went straight to Ishi. "We need to talk."

Ishi followed Oslo into an alcove. Oslo turned, his expression concerned, or as concerned as a robot could be. He lowered his voice. "They are scouring the island for you children. They have robots watching the docks for when the boat arrives. I think they suspect what we are doing."

Ishi's heart fell. How would they get out, now? He thought about their escape plan and what else they could do. They'd need a diversion to be able to get to the boat safely. "I'll do something."

"What?" Oslo asked.

"If I can distract the robots, can you get the children onto the boat?"

"Without you?"

Ishi nodded. "It's the only way, I think. Unless you have a better idea?"

Oslo shook his head. "No, but what happens once we are on the boat? What about you?"

"Can the other robots swim?"

"Not that I know of. Not these robots, anyhow. We are made of old parts. We rust."

Ishi chewed his lip, considering their options. "Okay, so I'll call out from the woods and get the robots to come after me. You load the children on the boat and get it out onto the ocean. I'll swim for it."

"Can you swim?" Oslo asked, surprised. Ms. Virginia had always forbade the children from going into the water.

Ishi began to smile. "Our little secret. I taught myself when I was supposed to be collecting rocks for the gardens. I couldn't resist. It made my leg feel better."

Oslo's eyes shined bright. "You are a leader, Ishi. You have always challenged things that did not make sense. You may be our only chance."

Ishi beamed with pride. He appreciated Oslo saying so. "I think I knew I didn't belong here. I thought it was because I was getting older and would be sent away, but now I understand I was meant to go back to the world to change things."

Oslo shifted to face the space with the other children. "We need to go. Are you ready?"

"Yes. We can hide in the woods until the boat comes. If you can take the children to the brush on the far side of the dock, once we see the boat come in, I'll distract the robots from the wood line and lure them over. I should be able to circle back as you move out into the water and dive in. They can't follow me out there."

Oslo went with Ishi into the room and they told the children their plan for escape. The children looked to Ishi for confirmation, still not knowing how much they could actually trust Oslo.

Ishi reached out and held Oslo's hand. "Oslo is one of us. We need him to do this. Trust me. Trust him."

They nodded, their faces still unsure. Jai spoke up. "What if it doesn't work? What if we get caught?"

Ishi sighed. "If we get caught, we're dead. There's no way Ms. Virginia would let us live after all of this. So, it needs to work."

Fear crossed their faces but they agreed to the idea. Using the dirt on the ground and a stick, they drew out the plan, going over any contingencies. If Ishi was unable to divert the robots, Oslo and the children would return to the space. From there, they didn't have an alternative but figured they could hide in the space for a while before it was found.

At the designated time, the group slipped up into the boat house and scanned around the area. They were close enough to the dock to see four robots, one stationed on each corner of the dock. The boat was coming in, so Oslo led the other children behind the boat house, through the woods, to the brush on the other side. Ishi held his breath, praying he would be brave enough to do what needed to be done.

The image of the woman in his dream popped to mind and her kind face gave him the courage he needed to push himself forward. He hurried through the woods to the other side of the dock, not trying to be secretive. One of the robots on the dock turned at the sound and alerted the other robots. They all spun to see what made the ruckus as the boat eased up to the dock. Ishi knew it was now or never, but was aware he couldn't make it obvious he was trying to get their attention, so he pretended to trip and fall, crashing into branches and leaves beneath him.

Two of the robots dashed off the dock toward him, but the other two stayed put. Ishi cursed under his breath as he got up and ran, forcing his twisted leg to keep up. The two were close on his heels, but the other two were still standing guard. What would Oslo do now?

Oslo came out of the brush without the children and approached the dock. The other two robots turned to see him approaching and told him to halt. Oslo kept advancing on them, pointing into the woods.

"I found the other children, they are this way!"

One of the robots came off the dock, as the boat crew unloaded the supplies and hauled them onto land. Oslo kept pointing and gesturing to the robot coming his way and the robot went into the forest in search of the children. The last robot didn't budge, however.

Ishi circled back through the woods with the other two robots close on his tail, his leg aching and dragging him down. If Oslo and the children didn't move fast, he'd be caught. He stumbled and went to a knee, then forced himself back up. Out of breath and energy, he pushed on, hearing them right behind him. Deciding he didn't have a choice, Ishi darted for the water, knowing it was his only chance to escape the robots.

As his feet hit the water, he saw Oslo do something unexpected on the dock. The small robot ran full force at the last remaining robot, knocking it into the waves. Ishi paused in shock as Oslo motioned to the hiding children and yelled, "Come!"

This snapped Ishi out of his stupor and he dove into the ocean as the children scrambled on board the boat. Oslo untied the boat and pushed it away from the dock. It was left idling by the boat crew, so once it was away from the dock, Oslo was able to steer it into the water.

Ishi dug deep for his energy reserves and began swimming as hard as he could to the retreating boat. The robots after him stopped at the water's edge, unable to pursue him into the ocean. Even though he was no longer being chased, he faltered, unable to swim anymore.

The waves overtook him and he found himself slipping under, his muscles spent. He was relieved to see Oslo had safely gotten the children onto the boat and away from the dock, but knew he couldn't join them, allowing the water to drag him down.

Ishi thought of the woman, his mother, and hoped he'd find her when the last of his breath left his body. He breathed out, ready to let the water in when he felt something grab him and yank him up. As his presence came back to him, he realized he was being dragged onto the boat by Oslo and Jai. They laid him on the deck and hovered around him. Ishi put his hand in the air.

"Alive," he muttered between gasping breaths.

Timmy and Dari cheered, hearing his voice, and ran over, clinging to him. Oslo guided them back.

"Let Ishi catch his breath. But hurry, Ishi, because I don't know how to drive a boat."

"I'm not much better," Ishi whispered.

They helped him to his feet and sat him in the captain's chair by the steering wheel. Ishi glanced around to get his bearings and placed his hands on the wheel. There was a map in front of him and he squinted at it. It clearly showed the mainland with coordinates. He wasn't sure that's where they were going but shrugged, guiding the boat in that direction.

Oslo came up beside him, wiping salt water off his arm. "Glad you made it, Ishi."

Ishi smiled up at his friend and nodded. "Not without your help."

Oslo patted Ishi on the shoulder, then went back to the other children. Ishi couldn't stop grinning and focused on the vast ocean before him. No matter what happened, the island was growing smaller behind them.

They were on their way.

# Chapter Twelve

The ride was silent for some time, each of the children taking in the experience around them. While they'd all been close to the ocean being on the island, riding in the boat *on* the water was a completely different reality. Dari let his hand hang over the side, feeling the water rushing through his fingers with a big grin. Ishi stayed focused on directing the boat but noticed Jai staring off, her face twisted in concern.

"Jai, are you alright?" he asked.

She turned her head toward him and shrugged. "I guess. Glad to not be on the island anymore."

"Why do you seem sad, then?" Ishi prodded.

"Ishi, what do you think you'll find when you get to the mainland? Other than escaping, what is it you're seeking?" Jai inquired, her pointed chin trembling.

Ishi thought about it. If he was being honest, he wanted to find his family. To be accepted and brought into people who loved and cared for him. However, he knew the chances of that were slim, so he at least wanted to get someone who could help them. Assist the other children on the island. Stop Ms. Virginia. "I don't know. Help?"

Jai scowled at him. "Don't lie, tell me what you really, really hope will happen."

"I guess... I know it sounds silly, but I'd like to find my family," Ishi answered quietly, ashamed at his desires.

Jai stood up, adjusting her steps to the movement of the boat, and came toward him. "It's not silly, but it's also not likely."

Ishi felt shame and anger wash over him. "You don't know! They could be out there. Why are you so cynical?"

Jai sat down next to him and gazed across the water. "Because I can find my family, but they don't want me. You at least have something to wish for."

Ishi understood. Jai was different from the rest of them. She knew her family. Well, her mother, at least. There was no pot of gold at the end of the rainbow. She was going toward nothing. Ishi glanced at Jai, her bony shoulders hunched to her chest as if she was suffering a silent pain.

"I'm sorry. What do you want to find going back?" he questioned.

Jai stared at him, her eyes flashing with anger. "I'm not trying to find anything. There's nothing left for me there."

"Then why did you come with us?"

"What choice do I have? Stay on the island where children are being picked off one at a time? I'll take my chances. Besides, I have something I need to do back where I came from."

Ishi frowned. "What's that?"

Jai smiled as if she had an amazing secret and shrugged. "Kill my mother."

Ishi's hand slipped off the steering wheel, causing the boat to jerk slightly to one side. He grasped the wheel again and righted it. "What?"

"You heard me."

They sat staring at each other for a moment when Oslo came up. He glanced at the dashboard and frowned. "Ishi, we may run out of fuel. They only go back and forth to the closest location, but since we are going up the coast, we may need more gas."

This distracted Ishi from Jai and he looked at Oslo, his brows knitted. "How far can we get?"

"Maybe a little further than where they go."

"Shouldn't we go there, instead, then travel on foot?" Ishi asked.

"We could, but they would have reported the boat stolen by now. They will be looking for us."

Ishi hadn't thought about that and felt his stomach clench. The idea of the mainland was all make-believe to him, anyway, having never seen it. Or, not remembering seeing it. Of course, they'd be searching for the stolen boat.

He chewed his lip and thought about what they could do. "What if we steal another boat?"

Oslo nodded. "We could if we can find one, however, most are locked up when no one is on them. We can plan to go as far as this boat will take us, then look for another boat. Or try to go on foot, but I fear we would be obvious. Four children and a robot."

Ishi pictured it and almost laughed. Him with his twisted leg, blind Darius, pale Timmy, angry Jai, and a piece-mealed robot. Yes, they would stick out. They couldn't split up either, they needed each other to survive. He rubbed his forehead, the thoughts weighing him down.

"I guess we'll just head up the coast and see what happens," he muttered.

Oslo didn't respond but headed to the back of the boat where Timmy was sitting on a bench. The boy was taking deep breaths, or trying to. Oslo sat with him and placed his hand on the boy's back, whispering gently to him. Timmy nodded and continued to breathe as deeply as he could. Ishi knew this wasn't good, the escape had put stress on Timmy's heart. Oslo glanced at Ishi, then back at Timmy. He was worried. As was Ishi. Like Darius, Timmy was his little brother and he didn't want anything bad to happen to him.

It was evening before they could see the lights off the mainland. Even then, they were way off in the distance. The children were mesmerized. Even Jai. Though she'd come from the mainland, she'd never seen it from this side. They watched the lights flickering on the horizon in awe, Timmy describing the sight to Dari.

Oslo came up to Ishi. "We need to cut the engine and drop the anchor."

"Why?" Ishi replicd, confused.

"A boat coming in at night will set off alarms and draw unneeded attention to us. Besides, we must rest. If we cut the engine and lights, no one will know we are out here. We can get up early before the sun and head that way. For now, you must sleep."

Ishi wanted to argue, but he knew Oslo was right. They would be obvious coming in at night. His eyes were also heavy and his limbs exhausted. He cut the engine and Oslo assisted him in releasing the anchor, making sure it was stable. Once they did that, the group went down into the boat's cabin. They were happy to find tins of food and a loaf of bread. Ishi sorted food out and handed each of the children a plate. Dari and Timmy ate with their heads bent close together, whispering some secret. Jai took her food and went back up to the deck. Ishi made himself a plate and went to the other side of the cabin to be alone. He was tired and didn't feel like talking to anyone.

After they all ate, Ishi tucked the two boys into bed, which was only a bedroll on the floor. He checked on Jai, who'd found a book on constellations and was reading it in the corner. He nudged her with his foot and smiled.

"I'm glad you came along, Jai."

Shoving away her sour mood earlier, Jai smiled at him. "I am too, Ishi. I'm sorry about before."

"For what?"

"For saying I was going to kill my mother."

Ishi tipped his head. "I know you're frustrated and it's okay to imagine doing that to work through your feelings about what she did to you."

Jai chuckled, then shook her head. "Oh, no, I *am* going to kill her. I just meant I was sorry for surprising you with that information."

Ishi watched her for a moment but could tell she was serious. He reached out and touched her head. "Thanks for trusting me."

A genuine smile crossed her mouth. "I do trust you. You and Oslo."

"I trust you, too, Jai. I'm... I'm really sorry about what your mother did."

"She will be, too," Jai replied, going back to reading.

Ishi could feel the rage simmering beneath her calm exterior and knew she meant it. He hoped for her mother's sake, they never ran across her, however, he had a feeling Jai would find her, no matter what. He shuddered and went to find Oslo.

The robot was up on deck, gazing out across the black sea. Ishi sat down next to him and cleared his throat. "Oslo, promise me something."

Oslo turned his round eyes on Ishi and cocked his head. "I can try."

"If something happens to me, get Timmy, Jai, and Dari somewhere safe."

Oslo nodded, then shifted his eyes back to the water. "I will do my best. I am worried about Timmy."

Ishi was, as well. "Is he getting worse?"

"He goes in cycles, however, out here he is struggling more than usual."

"Why?"

"Stress, maybe. Or simply bad timing," Oslo explained.

"Can we do anything for him?" Ishi asked.

"Not that I can think of. As he grows, his heart is under more pressure to keep up. He needs a real doctor."

A real doctor. Ishi didn't know how they could get Timmy to one, but maybe once they reached the mainland, they could find one. Ishi hated Ms. Virginia even more. She'd let the boy die just to sell him off in pieces. They didn't stand a chance on the island. Getting to the mainland was their only hope, albeit slim.

He glanced at Oslo. "Why aren't you like the other robots? How are you able to understand our feelings and what we're going through?"

Oslo stared at him for a moment, then back at the ocean. "Evolution."

Ishi didn't understand. "How does a robot evolve?"

"Everything can evolve. By exposure to different realities and ideas, we can grow."

"But you are made of parts constructed by man. Aren't you only able to understand what man puts in you?"

Oslo chuckled and shook his head. "The parts are made by man, much like your own. However, my soul is my own."

His soul? Ishi couldn't comprehend. "You have a soul? Where did it come from?"

Oslo waved his hand around him. "Everywhere, nowhere. Where does your soul come from?"

Ishi thought about it and didn't have an answer. Much like Oslo, his body was created by man but his soul came from elsewhere. He rubbed his nose. "I don't know. It's been there since I was born, I think. My body is here, but my soul has always been."

Oslo's eyes shined like bright, peridot beacons and he bobbed his head. "See?"

For the first time in his short life, Ishi truly did.

# Chapter Thirteen

"**L**and!" Timmy's voice was weak but excited as his thin finger pointed toward what they were all hoping to see.

Off in the distance, a shape crept up from the water. It grew larger as they drew closer. Eventually, the group could make out the outlines of tall buildings. Ishi's heart pounded in his chest as it dawned on him this nondescript mass could hold all the answers to his questions. The younger boys squealed with excitement, while Jai stared warily at the approaching landform.

Ishi eyed Oslo to get a read on the robot's interpretation, but Oslo simply observed the land in the distance. Finally, he rotated to Ishi and motioned to the right. "We need to go over there. Not too close to the land."

Ishi was about to protest, knowing they were all tired of being on the boat and were ready for the next leg of their journey. Then he remembered what Oslo said about them being looked for. It wasn't safe to go to the closest port. They needed to go up the coast to an area they theoretically weren't being searched for. Ishi knew the boys would be disappointed, but their safety was more important than their desires. Ishi followed Oslo to the mounted map.

"Here, this is where we should go," Oslo instructed, pointing at an area on the map.

Ishi peered in close but couldn't tell any difference between here or there. "Why there, Oslo?"

Oslo glanced around at the other children, who were taking turns gazing through a telescope at the far-off land. Even Dari liked holding the scope to his unseeing eye. "This area is still held by the Maboni. Maybe not for long, but they will help us if they can."

Ishi was still unsure about the Maboni, the Raiders, and their true intent but Oslo seemed comfortable with them. Ishi considered that since Oslo was created by Raiders to begin with, he might be biased. If robots could be biased.

"What if we get there and they're gone?"

Oslo turned to Ishi. "They will not be."

"How do you know?"

"I just do," Oslo replied, his large eyes shining in the light. Ishi couldn't help but believe him.

They shifted direction to skirt the coastline, causing Timmy to stare at them, confused. Darius, sensing the shift, called out.

"Where are we going?" his small voice asked, cutting above the sound of the boat's engine.

Knowing it was better to be upfront with the other children, Ishi called them over into a huddle to let them know the plan moving forward. Jai trailed behind, clearly unhappy with the whole ordeal. Once the group was around him, Ishi showed them their voyage on the map, speaking aloud for Dari as he drew his finger along the map.

"We need to stay away from anywhere they might know we stole the boat and will be searching for us. Oslo says there is a safe place up the coast, so we're heading there," he explained. "There are people who can help us."

"Why would they do that?" Jai spat, her words tired and frustrated.

"Because they are like you," Oslo answered her before Ishi could.

"How?" Timmy chimed in.

"They were driven from their homes, abused, and some were killed," Oslo replied.

"So, why would they want to help us?" Jai questioned, not believing a word Oslo said.

Oslo didn't answer right away, his focus on the map. When he spoke again, his voice was gentle, pained. "You do not have to believe me, but I know what I know. Not every human is bad. Some want the world to be like it was. A place for everyone. These people were left with nothing, yet they kept what was most important."

"What, Oslo?" Jai asked, her voice teetering on hope, yet too jaded to totally let it in.

"They believe everything we need in this world is all around us. That the land and one another provide everything we need."

The children were silent, absorbing Oslo's words. Their lives taught them nothing they needed was around them. No one to depend on, nothing to eat, no comforts of any kind.

Oslo's words felt flat. How could anyone treated so poorly, trust anything was for them?

Jai turned on her heel and stormed to the back of the boat, her arms crossed in anger. Oslo followed her and Ishi came up behind.

"Jai, you have every right to feel the way you do. I know what I am saying makes little sense, but I promise there are people who care about you, even though they have never met you," Oslo said.

Jai stared at Oslo, her face twisted in rage. She stomped her foot and spun away. Oslo held his ground and placed his hand on the girl's back. Ishi expected her to lash out at the robot, but instead, she turned and clung to his metal frame as if she were drowning.

She sobbed into his chest. "Why?"

Ishi stood frozen, not sure what to do.

Oslo gathered the girl in his arms and sat on the bench with her. "Some people are simply broken, they have bad parts. No matter what you do, you cannot fix them."

Ishi understood. They were talking about Jai's mother. Ishi could still hope his mother was out there searching for him. Wanting him. Jai knew her mother wasn't. The person she should've been able to depend on, to feel protected by, was the one to cause her pain. She had no one.

Jai let all the suffering she'd been bottling up pour out in Oslo's arms. She shook violently, unable to contain all the emotions. "I was a good girl. I wasn't bad, I promise!"

"I know you were. You did not deserve what your mother did to you. She was defective, not you. You need to see it was not anything you did," Oslo explained.

"I wanted her to want me... to love me," Jai whispered through her tears.

Oslo sighed and nodded. "You deserved that. You deserved much more than she could give to you."

"She was my mother! My mommy. Why wasn't I enough for her to love me?" Jai asked, her pain so palpable, Ishi had to look away.

"You have always been enough. She was too buried to see that. But you are a gift to the world," Oslo stated as if this was written in stone.

Jai stared at him, wanting to trust his words, but too afraid to let the walls she'd carefully crafted over the years come down. She sat back and wiped her eyes, retreating back inside herself. "Thank you, Oslo."

She got up and walked over to Timmy and Darius, who were still standing by the map. Timmy was telling Dari what the map showed and used his hand to guide Dari's fingers along the coast as he spoke. Jai slid between them and they drew her into the conversation.

Ishi sat next to Oslo, gazing across the glistening water. "That was kind of you to say to Jai."

"It is the truth. Jai's mother was clearly unwell and Jai did not do anything to warrant such abuse."

"Unwell? Like sick?"

"In a way, yes. In her brain," Oslo replied.

"How do you know?" Ishi asked, trying to picture Jai's mother in his mind. He couldn't, he kept seeing Ms. Virginia.

"Well... I cannot say I know for certain, but what mother who was well would treat their child in such a terrible way? It seems inconceivable."

Indeed.

Ms. Virginia was cruel, but she wasn't their mother. However, Jai's mother was her flesh and blood. Ishi couldn't imagine his own mother locking him away and starving him. Even Ms. Virginia fed them. Well, sort of, anyway. Enough to pass the inspector's scrutiny. So, perhaps that had nothing to do with care and more to do with whatever she was getting out of it. In no way, did Ms. Virginia ever treat them as if she valued them.

It was an awful lot to consider. Ishi thought about his feelings toward the other children and knew it was something divine. A loyalty, a drive to keep them safe. A need to prevent them from feeling unwanted. A radiating warmth that made him feel happy and a sense of belonging. He'd never do anything to hurt them and couldn't imagine his life without them in it. He watched the three children, knowing they all were bound by some unexplainable force. In their unique way, they were a family, despite not having families to call their own anymore.

Ishi faced Oslo, sensing the same warmth for the robot, a smile on his lips at the reality. Oslo glanced at the children, then back at Ishi, a deep understanding crossing his metal face. Ishi was going to explain all of what he felt to Oslo when the robot patted Ishi's chest and spoke.

"It is called unconditional love."

# Chapter Fourteen

At Oslo's guidance, they anchored overnight with the intent of going on land in the early hours of the morning. They'd made good time and Oslo said they were in a safe enough region. Enough. He didn't say safe, he said safe *enough*. This disturbed Ishi, but he knew they needed to follow Oslo's lead, as he was the only one of them who understood the dangers of their trek. They went to the cabin, exhausted.

The days on the boat had taken their toll and their food was basically gone. They'd doled it out to last, however, no matter how little they ate, the food went fast. Ishi bedded down next to Timmy, who seemed weaker than usual. He could hear Timmy's shallow breathing.

"Ishi, are you awake?" Timmy's voice cut through the darkness.

"Yeah, Timmy?"

"Can you keep a secret?"

Ishi rolled over to face Timmy, barely able to make out the boy's outline in the dark. "Of course. Is everything alright?"

"I don't know. Sometimes I feel like I'm leaving my body. Like I'm here, but my soul is slipping out. Does that make sense?" Timmy asked.

Ishi had no words to reply. What Timmy was telling him was scary and he feared it was foretelling Timmy's future. Ishi couldn't bear the thought of losing his little brother, but Timmy was saying it without fear.

Timmy put his hand on Ishi's arm. "It's okay. I'm ready if it happens."

Ishi choked back a sob. "I'm not. We'll get to land and find you a doctor. There has to be something we can do."

Timmy let his hand slip back to his side, then sighed into the inky air. "Maybe. At least you are trying. Ms. Virginia said there was nothing that could be done. You know what she told me?"

Ishi shook his head, then realized Timmy couldn't see him in the dark. "No. What did she say?"

"She told me dying was my destiny. That my body would be used to save others. My organs."

Ishi sat up so fast, he almost lost his balance. "What do you mean? What was she going to do to you?"

He felt Timmy sit up next to him. The fragile boy coughed, then leaned against Ishi. "She said it was my time and I'd been chosen."

"For what?"

"To be sacrificed. She told me that me and Darius were sacred and needed to give our lives to save others."

Ishi wanted to vomit. He knew children went missing and Ms. Virginia had something to do with it, but hearing the words felt unreal, like a waking nightmare. "Did she say how or when?"

"She said I wouldn't feel much. Just a prick of a needle and I'd go to sleep. Then, I'd go to another world and my body here would be used to help other people."

Pushing aside his own disgust, Ishi took shallow breaths and imagined what would happen. What was happening to other children. Finally, he squeaked out, "Why? Why would she do that?"

Timmy squeezed his hand. "Knowing Ms. Virginia, I don't think she cared about other people, so she must've had another reason."

Rage filled Ishi and he broke his promise to Oslo to trust him, jumping up and darting out to the deck to confront the robot. Oslo was powered down in the seat by the steering wheel when Ishi rushed him, banging on the robot's round chest. Oslo's eyes came on, gradually gaining brightness.

"Ishi, what is it? Is everything alright?"

"No! Everything is *not* alright! I need you to tell me everything you know about the island, Ms. Virginia, and us. I know you looked through her files. What is the purpose of the island? Other than to put us out of sight."

Oslo waited to fully power back up then motioned Ishi to go with him to the back of the boat. Ishi followed impatiently, tired of not knowing what was going on. Oslo sat down at the back bench and Ishi sat next to him.

"Oslo, no more secrets. I need to know everything you know," he insisted.

Oslo nodded. "In order to comprehend what is happening on the island, you need to understand the reality around us. You have no memory of it, but it is a hard world. Jai has some experience in it, but even she was shut away from many of the laws."

"Laws? Like rules?" Ishi responded.

"Yes. See, the world changed many years ago. People became very greedy. So selfish, they began to lose their sense of humanity. As I spoke about, the indigenous people were the only ones trying to keep the land from falling into ruin. In response, they were driven from their homelands. The rest of the population eventually caused so much destruction, they were harming themselves. So, they created many laws. Laws against being poor, being different, being compassionate even. People were locked in camps, however, as time went on, the government did not want to pay for those people, so they found ways to incentivize the extermination of certain people."

Ishi couldn't stop the waves of horror washing over him, but he'd asked and now he needed to learn it all. "Different like me and Timmy?"

"Yes, and Darius. Different like the children on the island. Each of you was given to Ms. Virginia as her wards. The work you do pays some of your fees."

"Our fees? For what?"

"To exist. In a way, you are the lucky ones. Some children are killed immediately for their body parts. Children who cannot work. Adults too. All of the children in camps when they turn sixteen. Children eat little, adults eat a lot."

"What do they do with the body parts?" Ishi asked, not really wanting to hear the answer.

Oslo drummed his fingers on the bench. "See, in the world, there are those that make the decisions, control everything. They are above it all. The body parts are sold for their survival whether they directly need an organ or want to make elixirs out of them."

"What do you mean, elixirs?"

"Oh, like mixtures, potions. Some of them believe the organs of children, even babies, will give them a longer life."

Ishi felt the bile rise in his throat and didn't stop it when his dinner came back up. He leaned over and let the contents of his stomach empty onto the wooden deck. Oslo held him and assisted when he was done to get Ishi back upright. Ishi steadied himself. "Okay, what else?"

Oslo waited a moment, then continued. "Even though they do horrific things, the reason they have the camps is when they first were going to kill different children, some of society insisted they have guidelines. To prove they were doing a humane thing."

"A humane thing? Killing babies and children? How is that humane?" Ishi spat.

"If people make boundaries, they are convinced what they are doing is not so bad. They think it proves intelligent design. That they are forced to make a choice for the betterment of society."

"What would happen if a child like Timmy was born to someone in power like that? Would they let him live?"

"No. They do genetic testing and if a fetus shows any signs of being different, they abort it. Even to the point of completely survivable differences."

"Timmy's family couldn't afford the testing?"

"No more than your family could afford to get you surgery, or Darius's family could fix his eyes. So, you were taken away and placed in a school, as they like to call it."

"But really a work camp. A prison. What about Jai's mother? She was obviously well-off."

"She was and considered a necessity to society. Entertainers are often placed in a higher level of society. Protected," Oslo explained.

"Why was Jai sent to the island, then?"

"Jai was sent there because her mother's place in society is more important than Jai's life to them. Her mother is mentally ill, but as long as she provides a service to the population, she will be protected."

"And Jai? Isn't she part of that higher level?"

Oslo shook his head. "If her mother had cared for her, then yes. Since her mother did not want her, Jai became one of us, instead."

Ishi liked how Oslo said *us* and not *you*. He was one of them. Ishi yawned, his anger settling, but he had so many more questions to ask. "Oslo, are there a lot more children like us out there?"

"Some, however, as society continues to refine its standards with genetic testing and culling as they call it, the numbers are dwindling. Their goal is to eventually eliminate anyone who does not fit in with their design."

"Won't they still need organs and other things?"

"That much is true, but they are getting those from other sources, as well as creating them."

"Other sources? Where?" Ishi felt the hair on his arms rise, suspecting it was something else horrifying.

"Well... Ishi, this is not pleasant information. Are you sure you want to hear it?"

Ishi didn't, but what choice did he have if he was going to face it all? "Yes."

"Alright. They get organs from people they imprison, sometimes for minor crimes. Poor people go missing all the time, as well. Also, there is the third way."

"Tell me."

"They *grow* people for organs."

Ishi jumped up and spun around. "They do what?"

"They do not consider them humans, since they never leave their incubators, but yes, they are living, breathing bodies."

That was all Ishi could take. He burst into tears, his fists clenched at his sides. Even if they made it to the mainland, it didn't sound like they'd find any help there. If anything, they'd probably be murdered and sold off for pieces. "Why did you allow us to come on this journey?"

Oslo watched Ishi, then tipped his head. "First, there are some people who are fighting for change, to bring back balance. They are not winning but are still trying by enacting laws. They are the reason you are even placed in the 'schools'. They need to hear your stories to understand what is really happening, which is why you need to go to the Council. They oversee the camps. Then, there are the Raiders. They are trying to take down the higher-ups. The government. There is now only one government, one language, and one set of laws made by the elite. That is where the Raiders are trying to overturn things. They are not unlike the others attempting to bring change, except they are doing one thing differently."

"What?" Ishi asked, feeling defeated.

"They are breaking into prisons, camps, schools, and the like, freeing those trapped there. They bring them back to their pockets of resistance to join them."

"They are? Is that why they came that night?" Ishi felt a spark of hope.

"It is. I will tell you something, but you must never tell anyone, not even the other children."

"I promise."

"I still have a chip in my head they can communicate with. I cannot communicate back, but they send me messages to let me know what they are doing and where they will be. I knew they were coming that night, however, they weren't able to break all the way in."

Ishi listened and stared out onto the moonlit sea. There were people out there trying to save them. A smile broke across his face, but it only lasted a fraction of a second before a bright light washed over them from across the water. Panic froze him as he realized a boat was approaching them with a spotlight. Despite their best efforts, they'd been spotted.

They were caught!

# Chapter Fifteen

W hat happened next was too fast and scary for Ishi to understand. Yelling was all around them and the other children woke up terrified and crying. Shadows boarded their boat and the children's heads were covered in fabric as they were snatched and carried off the boat. Ishi did his best to fight back, however, his captor was stronger than him and Ishi's arms were pinned to his side. He called out for Oslo but heard nothing in return. He felt the shift below him as they were moved from one boat to the other, then was shoved into a room under the deck.

A hand reached out for his and he recognized it as Jai's. He squeezed it and hoped Timmy and Darius were with them. A cough let him know Timmy was there.

"Ishi?" Dari's voice called out softly.

"I'm here," Ishi replied.

"What's happening?"

"I don't know, Dari. Is Oslo here?"

"No, I don't think so. Oslo?" Dari called out.

Silence greeted them and they felt the boat pull off as an explosion rocked the waters around them. The boat swayed violently, flinging the children onto the floor. They gathered themselves and drew closer to one another, waiting for their fate. Ishi took the hood off his head and peered around. The space was dimly lit, but he could make out blankets and pillows in the corner.

"You can take off your hoods, we're alone," he assured the other children.

"Not that it makes much of a difference," Darius mumbled as he yanked the hood off. Their captors obviously didn't know he was blind.

Timmy and Jai took theirs off, as well, and gazed around the space. Timmy reached out for Darius, who took his hand. They sat clutching onto one another as they dreaded where they were being taken.

"Who took us?" Jai wondered aloud.

Ishi shrugged. "I couldn't see anything. Oslo and I were talking when a bright spotlight blinded us from another boat. We didn't even have time to react before they were on board our boat."

"Oh. Did they take Oslo, too?" Jai asked.

"I'm not sure. I think they blew our boat up, so I hope so," Ishi answered, standing up. He made his way to the door and tried the handle. It was locked, as he suspected. The door had a small window he peered out of. It led to a thin, dark hallway and he saw nothing out there. He sighed and came back over to the group. "If they come, let me do the talking. I'll take the blame for our escape."

"No!" Darius cried out. "We're all in this together, Ishi. I'd rather die than go back. What happens to you, happens to me."

Ishi was touched, however, there was no way he'd allow the children to be punished for his plan. He went over and placed his hand on Darius's head. "Thanks, Dari, but you're my family. It means everything to me to get you to safety, if that's even an option anymore."

They fell silent, their ears straining for any sounds outside the room. At one point, Ishi swore he heard Oslo up above and hoped it was so. He worried Oslo might have been the reason they got caught. Oslo told him he had a chip in him and maybe they were tracked by it. Even so, he trusted his friend and wished he was alright.

They pulled the blankets and pillows out and made one big bed for all of them, though none of them could fall asleep. Darius began to sing, his voice high and sweet. He'd pause every now and then to catch his breath but his songs soothed them all with the rocking of the boat. They began to doze off a couple of hours later when they heard the door handle unlock.

Ishi jumped up, ready to shield the other children. The door swung open and a light flicked on. Ishi paused when he saw Oslo come in, being followed by a small, golden-skinned woman. Was Oslo being locked in with them? Ishi tensed and took a step forward when Oslo raised his hand.

"It is alright, Ishi. This is Pashmira. She is a friend. You are safe."

Ishi frowned at the petite woman, then cocked his head. "How do you know?"

"I work with them. These are the people who built me. Well, originally built me before Ms. Virginia piece-mealed me together."

"Oh. Uh... nice to meet you?" Ishi stammered. The woman seemed familiar to him, then he realized she looked sort of like him. Dark hair, tan skin, almost black eyes.

She nodded and put her hand out. "You are secure with us. We're sorry we had to transport you in such a scary way, but we couldn't let you see where we were going. Once we get to our island, we'll bring you out. Please, rest. We'll bring you food shortly. It's not much, but from what Oslo said you are used to, it will be good."

"Who are you?" Jai asked from behind.

"Well, we are people trying to set things right. Save the ones we can. You may have heard us called 'Raiders', however, we go by our original name of Maboni. We were driven from our land and have since taken over another island."

Oslo nodded, then waved his hand. "Rest, we will tell you more later. You are under the protection of the Maboni people. They are often under attack but will make sure you are as safe as can be. Ishi, can we speak for a moment?"

Ishi followed Pashmira and Oslo into the hallway. They shut the door behind them. Oslo motioned to Pashmira.

She glanced at the door, then back at Ishi. "I understand one of the children has a weak heart? We have doctors, though no way to perform surgery. We'd like to take him in and see if we can assist."

Ishi frowned. He didn't want Timmy going anywhere without him. "Why he can't stay with us and you help him that way?"

"We have resources. Other tribes we work with. I know it's hard to comprehend, however, we're a network and there are tribes with more access to medical care. I think they can assist the boy."

"Timmy."

"Yes, Timmy," she replied. "I promise, we want to save him. Oslo told me of that woman's plan for Timmy and what she did to other children. We aren't like that. We want to help him survive, but Oslo told me you are their leader."

Ishi shook his head. "I'm no leader, they are my family. I want what's best for Timmy, but he is attached to Darius."

Pashmira stared at Oslo, who explained. "Darius is the other young boy, who is blind."

"Oh, well, they can stay together. I don't think there is much we can do for blindness, however, we won't separate them if that's best."

Ishi was watching his family dissolve away from him and couldn't fight the tears running down his face. He wanted what was best for Timmy and Dari, but they were his only family. He wiped his cheeks, then nodded. "Okay. You have to promise to take the best care of them."

Pashmira did something unexpected and moved forward to wrap Ishi in an embrace. She stepped back, meeting his eyes.

"You are special. You *are* a leader, whether or not you believe it. Your love for these children is unprecedented. We will honor and care for them, as well. In the meantime, you'll be a guest on our island until the next leg of your trip We needed to blow up your boat, so they couldn't find you. When you are ready to go, we'll provide you with another boat. We'll discuss your plan and goal more in-depth once we get settled. If you feel you need to leave our protection, that is."

Now, Ishi wasn't so sure. If they were safe with the Raiders, should they go? He considered the options, then dropped his head. "I do. I need to get to the mainland and try to tell people what is happening in the camps. The truth. Change the course of things."

Pashmira glanced at Oslo, then back at Ishi. "I understand. Get some rest and tomorrow we'll bring you all into our forum. We make no decision without everyone's input. We want your input. As I said, you are welcome to stay with us, but if you go, we'll make sure you have what you need to continue your journey."

She smiled and wandered back down the hallway out of sight. Oslo turned to Ishi. "She is good. They lost everything when they were driven off their land. Her child was taken, as well. She told me she has some information about the word Palashtu that was in your record. She can tell you more, but it was another land the indigenous people were driven from like the Maboni. Your family was likely from there originally, though it did not say where you were acquired."

"Stolen," Ishi interjected.

"Yes, stolen," Oslo agreed. "Sleep, the sun will rise soon and we will arrive at their home. Food will be coming shortly. The door will remain unlocked. They locked it to make sure you did not get confused or hurt."

"Oslo?"

"Yes?"

"Have you been in contact with them all along? The Maboni?"

"Yes and no. I could hear their communications but could not communicate back unless I radioed, which I tried not to do, so they did not get tracked. But I did give them information about the island and the systems. I have been trying to save you all for some time."

"Did Ms. Virginia know?"

"If she knew, I would be scrap at the bottom of the ocean," Oslo answered honestly.

Ishi stepped forward and wrapped his arms around Oslo. "I don't know what I'd do without you."

Oslo rubbed Ishi's back and hummed gently. "I have loved you all since you came to the island. All of the children. I have grieved every single child Ms. Virginia killed."

Ishi stepped back, his eyes full of tears. "I hate her."

"Me too, Ishi."

"Ms. Virginia said robots couldn't feel love or hate," Ishi whispered.

"Oh, Ishi. Some robots have the capacity to feel those more than modern-day human societies."

"Are there more like you out there?"

"There are... and we are going to find them."

# Chapter Sixteen

A fter what may have been the heartiest meal the children ever ate, they were shown back to their space to rest. Due to having lived with empty bellies and fear most of their lives, all of them fell into a deep sleep and didn't wake up until the sun was high in the sky. When they awoke, Ishi could tell the boat engine was off and peered out a small window in the space. He could see land and from the way the boat moved, they were docked. His heart skipped in his chest. They'd slept all the way to the Maboni's island. He jiggled the door handle and as promised, it wasn't locked.

The other children began to stir and rub the sleep from their eyes. They stared at Ishi for assurance and he grinned.

"We are at the Maboni's island. They promised to protect us. Are you ready to go check it out?"

The two boys nodded, but Jai seemed unsure. Ishi knew her life had been nothing but unwelcome surprises and couldn't blame her. He went over and extended his hand to her. She bit her lip but took it. The group went out the door down the hallway, searching for Oslo and the way out.

As if he sensed them coming, Oslo stepped out from behind a corner, freshly shined and looking a little more put together. He moved toward them, his eyes bright and clear.

"I hope you got some rest?"

"We did. Can we go onto the island?" Ishi asked.

"Yes, but first, Pashmira would like to introduce you to the family. They have been anxiously waiting for you to awaken," Oslo replied and motioned for them to follow him.

They went down a series of halls and up a set of narrow metal stairs, leading to the ship's deck. Oslo led them to the front of the ship where a large group of people were gathered. They turned to watch the children approach, their faces warm and welcoming. As they drew closer, one of the women stepped forward with two hand-carved canes in her grasp. She handed one to Ishi and one to Darius. Since they'd both lost theirs, this was an appreciated gift.

"Children, welcome to our family. There are more on the island but this is our forum. We represent the tribes who have gathered together here to stand against oppression. Do you understand that word?" Pashmira asked.

While they had been educated on the island, there were certain things they weren't taught. One, being the state of the world, the other being what happened to many of the people. Ishi shook his head.

"Oppression is when one group of people exerts control over another and doesn't allow them the same rights."

"Like Ms. Virginia?" Ishi inquired.

"And my mother," Jai added bitterly.

"Yes. Those are both good examples of oppression on an individual basis. We are fighting systemic oppression, which means laws and policies are made to oppress a certain sect of people. Did you learn any history in your schooling?"

The children shook their heads. They were taught math and English and had approved books to read, but nothing that taught them about the world outside of the island. After all, they just had to pass tests, but Ms. Virginia didn't want them getting ideas. Not to mention, once they turned sixteen they were apparently killed, anyway. If not before.

"Well, that's more than we can cover now, but we'll start to teach you true history, current affairs, and how to fight," Pashmira said.

"How to fight?" Timmy squeaked out.

"You'll need to learn how to fight. In this world, there are many who want to take from you. You'll need to learn to protect yourself and your family."

Jai wrinkled her nose at the word family, but Pashmira came over and placed her hand gently on Jai's cheek. "That's not your family anymore. The children you came with are your family. Oslo is your family. *We* are your family, now. Family grows from love, everything else is a lie."

Jai's face lit up like Ishi had never seen. She was being promised something she'd never known. People who loved and wanted her around. He smiled to himself, also feeling the hope form in him.

Pashmira went around and introduced the rest of the forum, though Ishi lost track of their names. All of them bowed slightly, then touched the space between and a little above their eyes. When they were introduced to Darius, they did the same, but then also touched the same spot above his eyes. He giggled each time, making them chuckle, too.

After the introductions, the children were guided off the boat and led to a large, round building near the dock. Inside were chairs in a circle and each member of the forum took a seat, gesturing for the children to join them. Once all were seated, a slender man named Ravi stood up.

"Welcome to the tribal forum. Today we welcome our esteemed guests, Ishi, Oslo, Jai, Timmy, and Dari. Ishi also known as Ishmael, Timmy also known as Timothée, Dari also known as Darius. Jai also known as Jai," he teased with a wink, causing a titter to run through the group. Jai blushed, grinning.

"As long as you are with us, we will protect and care for you. However, we will never ask your allegiance as that is only yours to decide."

"Allegiance?" Timmy muttered in response.

Ravi smiled with a nod. "Allegiance means you decide you want to be with us, to be one of us."

"Oh," Timmy whispered.

"You are always welcome here, allegiance or no. The only thing we ask of you is secrecy and for you to contribute your skills while you are with us."

"What kind of skills?" Ishi asked.

"Whatever you have to offer. It could be a language, or cooking, or gardening, anything really," Ravi explained.

"I can cook," Ishi offered.

"I know computers," Timmy chimed in.

Darius cocked his head as he thought. Then he smiled and opened his mouth. The most beautiful song came out of his small body and many in the group gasped. He paused. "I can sing if that's something?"

Pashmira went over and embraced him. "That is everything!"

Jai sat quietly, her mouth turned down. "I have nothing to offer."

Pashmira shook her head. "I doubt that. You were simply never allowed to figure out what you are good at. Take your time and explore here. We'll have you join us in tasks and maybe you'll find your special skill."

Jai looked doubtful but didn't argue. She chewed her fingernails and watched Pashmira. Ishi reached out and took her hand. The rest of them had been a sort of family on the island, now Jai needed to believe she was, as well.

"There's one more thing we'd like to discuss, as we feel it may be critical. We'd like to have our doctor look over Timmy. Well, we'd like our doctor to give you all an examination, but we feel Timmy's heart condition may need extra care as soon as possible. Timmy, would you be okay with staying overnight in our hospital?" Ravi asked.

Timmy appeared scared and glanced at Ishi, who nodded at him. The boy clutched Darius's hand before he replied. "Can Dari stay with me?"

"Of course. I promise nothing will hurt. Our doctor, Zelai, would like to track your heart for twenty-four hours and see if it is something we can address here, or if you might need more specialized care. Do you know anything about your heart, like how it got in this condition?"

Timmy shook his head, his eyes wide and round. Oslo spoke up. "According to his records, Timmy was born with a hole in his heart. His family could not afford the surgery to fix it, so he was taken from them and sent to the island."

"Ah. This is good information we will pass on to Zelai. Timmy, we don't want you to be scared. We're here to help. Outside of our island, we do have contacts on the mainland who secretly help us when they can. We may be able to get you assistance."

"What about me?" Dari questioned. "Can they make me see?"

Ravi and Pashmira exchanged glances, then Ravi turned back to Darius. "I don't think we have the technology for that, unfortunately. I'm sorry. However, Zelai will look at you, and see if there is anything we can offer to make your life easier."

Ishi knew better than to ask about his leg. Unless they could give him a new leg, there wasn't much to be done. He was fine with his reality and really wanted them to help Timmy and Dari. As for Jai, her injuries were mental and he hoped being in a loving, supportive environment would assist in her healing.

Darius was quiet as he absorbed what they told him, then smiled. "It's okay, this is the only way I know how to be, anyway. Save Timmy, that's all that matters to me."

After the group disbursed, the children were shown to small hand-crafted huts on the island. They were offered one each but they decided to pair off. Timmy with Dari and Jai with Ishi. Pashmira explained this was their space and the tribe had stocked the huts for them to enjoy.

The children stepped in and were surprised to see the huts were decorated with art, games, and books. There were bunk beds and a small table in each one. The bedspreads were hand-sewn out of colorful fabric with animals, nature, and fun shapes. It seemed almost magical as if it was made just for them. Ishi felt a part of him he'd never known react in delight. The little boy he once was, found a space he belonged.

On each table was a basket of fruit and baked goods. Jai ran over and shoved a purple orb in her mouth, grinning as the juice dribbled down her chin. Ishi grabbed one and took a small bite, in awe at the flavors exploding in his mouth. He'd eaten berries he found on the island but this was something new altogether.

"Do you know what it is?" he asked Jai, wiping the juice from his chin.

She side-eyed him and he felt embarrassed. Of course, she didn't. She'd been deprived of food more than the children on the island had. He shrugged in apology as she dug in the basket, taking out a handful of smaller green orbs. She waved them in the air with glee and threw one at Ishi, who caught it midair and popped it in his mouth. He crunched down, the orb coating his tongue with tart sweetness.

Jai spun around, her dress billowing out beside her. She tipped her head back, the happiest Ishi had ever seen her. She almost yelled when she replied.

"I don't know, but I am *never* leaving this place!"

# Chapter Seventeen

W ithin a week, the children felt like they'd found their new family, though Ishi knew it would be short-lived. He needed to find someone to appeal to in regard to the island and Ms. Virginia. Saving himself wasn't enough, he needed to go back and rescue the rest of the children. Stop Ms. Virginia from hurting anyone else. The Maboni wanted to help but admitted their small numbers could only temporarily stop the flow. Eventually, they'd be pushed back. They could stand up to Ms. Virginia. They couldn't take on the world... yet. Pashmira told Ishi they'd found friends in high places and were trying to create enough stir to change the way things were done in the world.

On the second day they were there, the children were given physicals and it was determined Timmy would need surgery to survive long-term. Zelai was working with her contacts to see about transporting him off their island to a surgical hospital. The rest of the children were given a clean bill of health, despite their existing issues. Jai was still malnourished and Zelai expressed she might always have problems due to being denied food for so long as she grew.

Darius was told there was nothing they could do to change his blindness, but Zelai made sure he was given tools to make his life better. Including a stack of books in braille and a translator where words could be typed or spoken in and translated to braille. On the island, he could only enjoy books if someone read to him, but Zelai explained there were many options created before the "Great Reform."

"What's the Great Reform?" Ishi asked her during his examination.

"There was a time when the world wasn't like it is now. When people took care of one another. Of course, there were always those who believed they were better than others and they complained and tried to change things, but never got much traction. Until the Great Reform. During that time, those people, the ones who didn't believe in equal rights, came together and started overthrowing governments. Putting their people in charge. It happened over a few decades, slowly at first, then very quickly as the power shifted."

"What happened then? Is that how we ended up on the island?" Ishi asked.

Zelai stretched his twisted leg out and rotated it to see how much flexibility he had. She was gentle, yet firm in testing the leg's limits. "Hmmm, I think you have a build-up of scar tissue. We can try some exercises to break through some of it, but surgery might also be an option."

Ishi didn't want surgery. "I'll try exercises. What happened next?"

Zelai eyed him and sat back. "Well, as I said, they put people in power who aligned with their beliefs. Some of those beliefs were that poor people, people with medical needs, people with differences, etc., didn't deserve the same rights as others. That's when the laws began to shift. It became a crime to be poor. Not outright, but if they could find a reason to lock poor people away, they'd do it. If someone couldn't pay their bills or became a burden to society, they would get locked up. No longer just murderers and rapists, now if someone fell behind on their house payment, their home would be seized, their children taken away, and they'd be put behind bars. "

Ishi listened, fascinated. "Because I was hurt as a child, I was taken away from my family?"

Zelai nodded. "Yes. It happens a lot. Once everything was moved to the private sector and people realized they could make money off imprisoning people and driving them from their homes, it happened very fast. Your family couldn't pay your medical bills, so you were taken away. Put on the island for a stipend."

"A stipend?"

"That's money for something. In your case, they take taxpayers' money to house you on the island. In turn, you work and exist to appease their guilt. However, no one feels guilty when adults are murdered, so they kill off the children once they hit sixteen, by putting them in work camps until they drop dead from exhaustion."

Ishi had heard some of this but hearing it again made the hair stand up on his arms. "That's horrible."

"It is and we have intercepted boats taking the sixteen-year-olds to the camps, but not enough. See, this all started in one country, then spread across the world. Where there used to be many countries and governments, now there is one system that makes all the decisions. A collective of people who don't look very much like us," Zelai explained.

Ishi pictured green and blue people for some reason, but he knew what she meant. "People more like Ms. Virginia."

"Exactly. And a lot of robots. They do the dirty work humans don't want to."

"Oslo is different, though."

"Indeed he is, Ishi. Oslo was created by those like us. To be a friend to humans. Most are programmed as nothing more than henchmen to the elite," Zelai said, motioning for Ishi to stand.

Ishi got off the table and stood as Zelai checked his leg. "What does that mean? Henchmen?"

"Oh. The robots are there to do whatever the humans say for them to do. Sometimes, it's only chores and the such, but the humans created an army of robots designed to kill and maim."

The more they talked, the more Ishi couldn't wrap his brain around what she was telling him. He'd seen Moscow and the other robots on the island do Ms. Virginia's bidding, however, he couldn't imagine a whole army of them doing humans' bidding. "Why?"

"Why robots, or why are they doing that?"

"Both," Ishi answered.

"Control, obedience. A robot doesn't require food or compassion, so they can make them work around the clock. Most robots don't have the ability to question their orders, so they are subservient on every level."

"Oslo said robots have the ability to feel things. Why don't the other ones?" Ishi asked.

"That's a good question and I think I know the answer. When you were on the island, you only understood the things you were shown, correct?"

"I guess."

"That's the key to control. Only give those you want to keep under your thumb the information they need to function, but never enough to make them think. That's what they do with the robots. If one starts to question, they break them into spare parts."

Ishi remembered the robot parts in the woods on the island. He wondered if they had challenged Ms. Virginia. Then there was Oslo. Why hadn't Ms. Virginia broken him into parts?

As if Zelai knew what he was thinking, she smiled. "Oslo is very special. He was designed to continue to evolve. Part of that evolution was awareness. He understands how he needs to act around different people."

"So, Oslo can analyze a situation and respond accordingly?"

"Exactly!" Zelai replied. "He's more like a human than a robot. Our hope is to take what we know about Oslo to turn the army of robots. Introduce compassion and understanding to their programming, so they don't just blindly follow orders."

"Is that even possible?" Ishi questioned doubtfully.

Zelai shrugged and gestured for him to take a seat. "Anything's possible. It might not be easy, but if we can find a way to mass program their systems, it's certainly doable."

Ishi sat as Zelai scribbled some notes on a pad. She drew out a small jar and handed it to him. "Rub this on your leg every morning and night. It may give you some more flexibility in that leg. If nothing else, it will ease the pain some."

"What is it?" Ishi asked, turning the jar over in his hands. He opened the lid and breathed in. It had a pleasant, earthy smell.

"A mixture of plants and other natural things from the land. One of the things we have done as a tribe is to continue to share our ways and our knowledge. My grandmother handed this recipe down to me from her mother and so on. We have been recording as much as we can to keep our history alive. Even when they kill us."

Ishi clutched the ointment and stared at Zelai. Even though they knew they might die, it was more important to not let their history die with them. He felt like he was holding gold. "Thank you, Zelai. Can you teach me one day about this? About any recipes you have?"

Zelai smiled and placed her hand on the side of his cheek. "I'd be honored. You know, Ishi, Oslo told me about what he saw in your records. You are destined for great things and I'd like you to join us in changing things. I know you need to get back to the island to save the other children, but so you know, there are islands like that one all over the world."

"Are they always islands? I mean, do they have camps or schools in other places, too?"

"From what I know, it's islands because they can control who goes on or off them. For the children, anyway. The adults are locked in prisons, sold off to medical facilities, or killed on the spot, depending on their perceived value and the risk they bring to the powers that be."

"Oslo says they keep the children alive to convince themselves they aren't monsters," Ishi suggested.

Zelai watched him for a moment, then sighed. "To a degree, that's right. However, that's not all of it. Some of it's because they can charge people money for your care. Not that the money actually goes to your care."

Ishi could agree with that. Ms. Virginia gave them nothing more than what it took to keep them alive. She was keeping most of the money for herself. Then forcing them to work to sell things. When they couldn't work up to her satisfaction or got too old, she found another way to make money. Ishi understood what Zelai was saying. The other reason the children were kept alive for a while.

Their organs.

# Chapter Eighteen

The best-laid plans, or so they say. The children were woken up by explosions within a couple of weeks of being with their new friends. Ishi heard Darius crying out and rushed to the boy's side, clutching him close to his chest. Dari trembled like a leaf and dug his thin fingers into Ishi's forearms.

"What is happening, Ishi?" the terrified child questioned.

Ishi attempted to get his bearings and peered around. Jai had followed him to Timmy and Dari's cabin and stood still, gazing out of the door. Ishi raised his brows at her, but she shrugged in response. For the world blowing up around them, she remained strangely calm. A side effect of being abused by the person she needed to trust most in the world.

Ishi rose, Darius still clinging to him. Timmy sat wide-eyed in bed, his skin pale and sweaty. Ishi knew his heart couldn't take much more stress.

"It will be alright," he assured them as he made his way to the door, Dari's arms and legs wrapped like a pretzel around him. He prayed he was right.

Jai stepped aside and Ishi stared hard out through the doorway, trying to make sense of what was happening. Flashes of light and large booms were going off on the other side of the village and Ishi could see shadows running through the forest. Unsure if they should stay put or try and hide froze Ishi in place. All eyes were on him for an answer he didn't have.

He shut the door and instructed the children to barricade it with the beds. As they pushed everything they had against the door, they could hear the sounds of fighting drawing closer.

Timmy frowned. "What do we do, Ishi?"

"I don't know. I think the island is under attack from outsiders. Hopefully, they won't try to come here. Or if they do, the Maboni won't be far behind. Get in the corner away from the windows," Ishi instructed.

The children did as they were told and gathered in a shivering clump in the far corner of the cabin. Within seconds the fighting was right outside the cabins and Ishi saw a torch get thrown into Jai's and his cabin, sending it up in flames. Part of him wanted to dart out and try to extinguish it, but his rational mind told him there was nothing to save and they needed to stay put.

The door began to rattle and Jai stifled a scream, her feelings beginning to surface. Despite her years of trauma, she knew what was on the other side of that door was coming to hurt them. Ishi motioned for them to hunker down and hide as best as they could. However, whoever, or whatever, was outside wouldn't stop and the windows shattered around them as the cabin was breached.

The children were trapped inside, so when a torch flew through the window, setting the curtains on fire, Ishi knew they'd need to make a run for it. He shuffled the children to the door and peered out. The movement of bodies was all around them and he didn't know who was friend or foe. Taking the risk, he shoved the door open, grabbed Darius by the hand, and whispered for them to follow him.

The group pushed out into the night, quickly being surrounded by the clash of weapons, smoke, and yelling. Ishi scanned the area and saw an area of fallen trees in the woods they could hide behind. If they could get there before being caught. Jai met his eyes and nodded. They needed to get to the trees. He switched Dari's hand to Jai's and scooped Timmy up onto his back, hoping he had the strength in his leg to get them both to the wood line safely.

As soon as they began to run, Ishi heard a voice yell, "Don't let them get away! Kill them if you have to!"

That gave the children the motivation they needed and Ishi all but about forgot his twisted leg. He felt like he was flying as they booked it across the open field to the woods. Something whizzed by his ear and he heard Timmy groan.

"Are you alright, Timmy?" Ishi asked, not slowing his pace for anything.

"Yes, something hit me, but keep going!" Timmy yelled, grasping Ishi's shoulders with everything he had in him.

They made it to the trees when a large figure stepped out in front of them, stopping the children in their tracks. Ishi set Timmy down and tucked the boy behind him, as Jai and

Dari gathered around him. The figure came forward, the moon casting light on it.

A robot. Not like any robot Ishi had ever seen. It was huge and angry-looking. Unlike Oslo, this robot was designed with destruction in mind. Its arms ended in some sort of shooting device on one, and a bayonet on the other. The robot's face was all machine, not registering any form of emotion or compassion. It appeared soulless.

The robot came toward the children, raising the arm with the gun device. It was going to shoot them on the spot. Ishi felt his heart drumming in his chest and looked around for an escape. There was none. The robot's eyes turned bright orange and the lights on its chest pulsated in a mesmerizing rhythm as if it was using them to communicate. No orders were given, no chance to reason. The robot's arm stopped midair and the device at the end of the arm began to rotate. Ishi squinted, waiting for the pain to hit from whatever was about to come out of the device.

The pain never came.

A bolt of silver came from the right of them, making a direct path for the robot. It struck the monstrous machine, knocking it to its knees. That's when Ishi realized what he was seeing. Oslo.

His small, misshapen, misunderstood friend had come to their rescue. Or, was at least trying. As Olso knocked the robot off guard, Ishi picked up Timmy and yelled for Jai and Dari to follow him. Jai led Dari and the four made it to the hiding spot, crouching down behind the fallen trees. Ishi watched as Oslo attempted to stop the other robot. However, the diminutive robot was out-sized and out-weaponed. The robot stumbled to its feet and turned on Oslo, raising its weapons at the much smaller robot.

Ishi held his breath, not wanting to see his friend blown to bits. He motioned for the children to stay put, then glanced around, spotting a large stick. Shaking his head, he grabbed the stick and stood up, thinking himself mad for what he was about to do.

He ran, screaming at the large robot. This threw it off guard as it spun to see what was coming at it. As if it lost all patience, the robot seemed to do the human equivalent of a frustrated sigh and point its weapon at Ishi. Ishi swung the stick as hard as he could, smacking the robot firmly on the shoulder. The robot didn't even move, however, Ishi's distraction gave Oslo enough time to come up behind the robot and jam a tool under its armor. The robot tried to face Oslo, but Ishi kept hitting it with the stick, causing it to focus on the boy.

Oslo ripped off a piece of the metal armor and shoved the tool inside the huge machine. A buzzing sound, followed by sparks, turned the monstrosity into nothing more than a statue. Ishi stared in amazement when Oslo snapped him out of his stupor.

"Run!"

Ishi did as he was instructed and bolted back to where the children were gathered. He hoped Oslo followed but when he looked back, he was alone. Oslo continued fighting. Ishi squatted down with the other children, praying their hiding place wouldn't be discovered.

The fighting seemed to go on forever and Ishi didn't know which side was winning. If there were more of the enormous robots, he feared the Maboni didn't stand a chance. He prayed he was wrong. Ishi focused on Timmy, who'd been abnormally quiet since they made it to the hiding place. Timmy was bent over and breathing funny when Ishi came to him. Ishi scanned Timmy's form to see if he could see an injury.

"Timmy? Where does it hurt?"

Timmy lifted his head, his chest heaving up and down in an attempt to catch his breath. He pointed to his side and Ishi could see blood seeping through the boy's clothes. He gently lifted Timmy's shirt and gasped at the wound on his side. Whatever had been shot at them passed through Timmy's body, but left some damage. In the dark, Ishi couldn't tell how serious it was but knew for Timmy everything was serious.

The sounds of fighting moved away from where the children were, and Ishi hoped the Maboni were alright. He could make out the colors of sunrise creeping into the sky and used the small amount of light to look for an escape plan. They were close to the dock, but that didn't mean there'd be a boat to take. He gestured for the children to stay put.

"Jai, keep an eye on the boys. I'm going to see if there is a way out of here. If you get discovered, scream as loud as you can. I'll find a way to get you," Ishi whispered.

Jai nodded, again abnormally calm. Darius sobbed quietly and Timmy curled into himself like a ball. Ishi felt guilty for leaving, but he needed to find an escape route for them. He shook his head and crept out of hiding. The battle was now going on in the main village area, so he headed in the other direction.

He passed the docks and as he suspected, the boats were gone. Possibly even sank by the attackers. He circled back and followed the sounds of fighting. As he came to the center of the the village, he could see the Maboni fighting with mainly robots, though it seemed some humans were directing the machines. He crouched down and observed, wondering what they'd do if the Maboni were defeated.

However, the Raiders held their own. Oslo stood with them, disarming the larger robots. He held a wand of some sort and when he got close enough, he'd jam it into the other robots and activate the tool. The wand tip lit up and sent energy into the robots, causing them to short-circuit. Ishi stared in amazement. Oslo, who was assigned to the children by Ms. Virginia because he was perceived to have little value, was single-handedly taking down an army of well-designed, armed to the hilt, killing machines.

Ishi knew he needed to get back to the other children and chewed his lip. He hadn't found a way to escape but he could see the Maboni were beginning to get the upper hand as the robots were systematically shut down. Ishi decided to go back and stay with the children until daylight. By then, he prayed the robots and the humans controlling them would be defeated.

As he headed to where the children were hiding, Ishi stumbled and fell over something large. He peered down and saw the body of Ravi, the slender, kind man who'd spoken at the forum. The man who'd welcomed them to the island.

Ravi's eyes were vacant and from the way his body was lying, Ishi knew he was dead. Sorrow filled his heart and he knew he needed to protect the children at all costs. Everything was life or death now.

There was no turning back.

Ishi ran as fast as his leg would let him back to the fallen trees. Jai was standing up, her eyes wide and terrified. Ishi drew closer, confused by her demeanor. She saw him and began to cry.

"Ishi! Help!" she cried out.

"What? What happened?" Ishi asked, ducking into the covering. He saw what she was yelling about before she spoke again and his stomach dropped. Jai grabbed his arm and pointed.

"It's Timmy! He's not breathing!"

# Chapter Nineteen

T he world seemed to move in slow motion as Ishi rushed to Timmy's side. The boy was still, his skin bloodless. Ishi wept as he gathered Timmy in his arms. He ran. He didn't know where or why, but he ran into the center of the village, yelling for help. Jai and Darius were close behind.

Pashmira, bloody and bruised, emerged from a hut. Seeing Ishi holding Timmy's body, her eyes grew wide and she began shouting orders. "Ben, find Zelai now! Timmy needs a doctor. It's an emergency!"

The man called Ben turned and ran, his focus on finding their only doctor. Pashmira directed Ishi to her hut and cleared the bed off for him to place Timmy down. Ishi ignored the streams of tears running down his face. Timmy was lifeless, his chest painfully unmoving. Pashmira began to perform CPR on the child, instructing Ishi how to help.

"Every time I motion to you, I need you to compress his chest thirty times, like this." Pashmira exhaled two big breaths into Timmy's mouth, then began compressions on his chest with her hands pressed together. "Got it?"

Ishi nodded and jumped in beside her. She'd breathe into Timmy, then motion for Ishi to do the chest compressions, counting them off as he did. They did this for what seemed like forever and Ishi was losing hope. Timmy remained still, his lips blue.

"It's not working!" Ishi cried out.

"Keep going. It might not seem like it, but this is keeping his body going. Zelai should be here soon," Pashmira replied, leaning in to breathe again.

Jai and Darius stood off to the side, clinging onto one another. Jai was telling Darius what she was seeing and the boy's face was stricken with fear. Hollering in the distance got their attention and Ishi peered out the window.

"Someone's coming."

Pashmira sat back, motioning for Ishi to compress again. "Keep going. Hopefully, they found Zelai. Everyone is scattered from the fighting."

"Did we win?" Jai asked from behind them.

"Win? No. But we chased the rest of them off. We lost some family, however, I think the rest are gathering back up. I only hope Zelai is one of them."

"Do you think she was killed?" Ishi asked, ignoring the shaking in his arms. What would they do if she was? She was Timmy's only chance.

"I don't know, Ishmael," Pashmira muttered, bending back down over Timmy to give him her breath.

Ishmael. No one had called Ishi that in his memory. Not since his mother. How did Pashmira know his real name?

He thought about that as he went back to performing the compressions on Timmy's chest. Pashmira reached out and placed her hand on his shoulder. Ishi met her eyes.

"You're doing good," she whispered, encouraging him to keep going.

Ishi bobbed his head and focused back on his task. "Did Oslo tell you my real name before we came? He was the only one who knew. Well... and Ms. Virginia."

"He did. I asked him to tell me everything about you children, so you knew we cared for you. It's a beautiful name. Did you know I had a son?"

Ishi didn't exactly. Oslo had told him she'd lost a child but not the details. He sat back and rubbed his arms when it was time for Pashmira to breathe into Timmy. When she was done and he started compressions again, she tipped her head, her eyes somewhere distant.

"His name was Karim."

"Where is... I mean, what happened?" Ishi asked.

"They took him. They took many of our children to try and break us. Change us. Erase who we are," Pashmira explained.

"Do you know where he is?" Ishi questioned, afraid of the answer but knowing what Oslo told him.

Pashmira checked Timmy's pulse and shook her head. "He's no longer on this plane of existence."

"He's dead?" Darius whispered from the corner.

"To this earth, yes. To me, no. They were transporting the captured children to another island, much like yours, when the boat sank, drowning them all," Pashmira replied, her words heavy with sorrow.

Ishi didn't know what to say and continued the chest compressions, trying to imagine what Pashmira's son looked like. He met her eyes. "How old was he?"

"He was four. I remember him crying out for me, reaching over the man's shoulders to try and get back to me. I was being held by a robot and I couldn't break free. It was the day my heart died. Now, I exist out of vengeance. I want them all to end. When I... when I heard about the boat sinking, I wanted to die. However, I knew the world was full of children like Karim, who needed to be saved. We tried to take over your island, but our attempts failed."

"Oh, that night the power went out?" Ishi asked.

"Yes. Unfortunately, the power was restored before we could get to you children. The Service has much more updated technology."

"The Service?" Ishi replied, not familiar with the term.

"So, the world government is run by a group called The Service. They are in charge of everything. Once every country had its own government, but those began to fall and The Service took over, combining all governments into one. Easier to control, harder for people to resist. They claim to serve the people, but they use The Guard to do their bidding. We never see The Service."

"The Guard is who came to take me from my home," Jai chimed in.

Ishi frowned, imagining what The Service looked like. He pictured people like Ms. Virginia sitting around a large round table, deciding everyone's fate. Pashmira felt for Timmy's pulse again and a brief smile touched the corners of her mouth.

"We have a light pulse. Barely there and thready, but that's encouraging. Keep going. Let me glance out to check if I see Zelai coming."

"If she isn't?" Ishi inquired.

Pashmira didn't look at him but put her hand in the air. "Let's just hope she is."

Ishi stared at his unconscious friend, his hands rhythmically doing what Timmy couldn't do on his own. Keeping his heart beating. Ishi closed his eyes and imagined Timmy's heart working on its own, hoping he was somehow sending a message to the organ. Pashmira made a sound with her mouth that sounded like a bird or small animal. She paused to listen, then grinned when the call came back to her.

"They found her! Keep going, Ishmael!" She came and sat down next to him in time to give the next round of air.

"Will he live?" Dari asked, his voice full of concern.

"Let's intend so," Pashmira replied. "Believe it."

The door flew open and Ben and Zelai rushed in, both worse for wear. Zelai had a bag and grabbed out a sort of stethoscope. She squeezed in between Pashmira and Ishi, listening to Timmy's chest.

"It's faint, but it's there. I'm about to give him something to strengthen the heartbeat. You can stop for now." She rooted in her bag and pulled out some tiny round tablets. She opened Timmy's mouth and placed them under his tongue. Then she inserted a needle in his arm, with a tub attached to a small bag.

"What's happening?" Dari asked.

"I'm giving Timmy some medicine. His body is very stressed. I can hear a heartbeat, thanks to Ishi and Pashmira, however, his heart isn't strong enough to keep going. We need to transport him out of here," Zelai explained.

"To where?" Ishi questioned, holding Timmy's hand in his own.

"I can't say as it's a secret network, but there are specialists who are trying to assist people who don't normally have access to medical care. I've already reached out, planning for Timmy to go in the next few days, but it's critical now. He needs to leave today."

"Will they save him?" Ishi asked.

"That's what we are trying to do. We have a boat at the dock now. Can you carry him, Ishi?" Zelai replied.

Everything was happening so fast and Ishi was afraid he'd never see Timmy again. He choked back a sob and nodded. Regardless of his feelings, Timmy needed surgery as soon as possible. If it wasn't already too late. He gathered the frail boy, who now felt like bones and air, following Zelai out. He paused at the door. "Wait, Darius needs to go with him."

Zelai glanced at Darius, then at Timmy. "Come on, then. Do you have your cane?"

"No, they burned it."

"We'll get you a new one. Let's go," Zelai instructed.

The group traipsed down a thin trail to the dock and onto the newly appeared boat. The Maboni must have hidden boats when they realized they were under attack. Everyone was crying on some level and Ishi felt like his heart was going to break. He placed Timmy on a bed inside the boat and kissed him on the head.

"Please, don't die," he whispered with intention into the boy's still face.

Darius climbed up next to Timmy and wrapped his arms around his friend. His brother. Ishi rubbed his head and smiled. "Timmy needs you, Dari. He can't be alone when he wakes up."

"If he wakes up," Dari replied, dejected.

"He will," Ishi assured, not totally believing his own words but needing to say them.

"What about you and Jai? Are you coming?"

Ishi bit his tongue, not wanting Dari to feel abandoned, but knowing he still needed to go and try to expose what was happening on the island. He sighed. "Dari, I need to go to try and get all the children help. I want to be with Timmy, and you, but if I don't go now, it will only get worse. I can ask Jai if she wants to go with you."

"I will go with you, Ishi," Jai stated from the door. "I can't help Timmy, but I can help you. Besides, I have something I need to do."

Something being killing her mother. Ishi watched her for a moment, then turned back to Darius. "You'll be safe with Zelai and the other doctors. Once Timmy is better, we will all be reunited again."

"You promise?" Dari asked.

Ishi didn't want to make promises he couldn't keep but right now that was the least of his concerns. "We are family. I promise."

Zelai came to the door and cleared her throat, her face twisted in worry. "I'm sorry, children, but if we are going to try and save Timmy, we need to go right away before we lose the slim chance we have left. Who's staying here, who's going with Timmy to the hospital?"

Ishi stood up, kissing Dari on the head. "If we can travel with you all, Jai and I will get off the boat at the next port. Dari is going to go with Timmy. Please let me know how the surgery goes, though."

Zelai nodded, knowing how hard it was for the children to be split up. "We will. Oslo still receives our signals, so we will send one once we know more. Ishi, can I speak to you outside alone?"

Ishi followed Zelai out and she faced him, her face lined with concern. "We're going to do our best, however, Timmy's in really bad shape. He might not make it through the surgery. He might not even make it to the surgery. I want to be honest with you, do you understand?"

Ishi didn't want to, but he did. "Yes."

"If Timmy doesn't make it, that will leave Darius all alone. We will care for him, but you are his family. How do you want to handle that if it happens?"

Ishi rubbed his nose, fighting back tears. He was the oldest, but still a child who didn't know how to fix everything. Or anything. He swallowed hard, tasting salt water tears trickling down his throat.

"Bring them both back to me. No matter what."

# Chapter Twenty

T he boat was prepared to take Timmy and Darius to the
hospital. Pashmira explained they had connections at a
major hospital that performed secret surgeries at night
for those unable or prevented from getting care. It was a
medical underground railroad of sorts. Jai and Ishi were able to
travel with them to the next port, then Timmy and Darius
would continue on. Ishi wanted Timmy to survive, but his
heart was breaking. They took off on the boat with Oslo and
Pashmira as their guides. Oslo would get off with Ishi and Jai,
and Pashmira would continue with the other two.

The mood on the boat was somber, not only because of
the children getting split up but also Pashmira and Oslo were
grieving the loss of their friends who died during the attack.
Ishi gazed out across the ocean, feeling out of sorts and lonely.
Oslo joined him and they sat in silence for some time. Finally,
Ishi turned to Oslo.

"What if Timmy doesn't make it?" he whispered.

Oslo met his eyes. "There is a chance he will not, but they are doing everything possible to save him."

"I know they are. What about Dari? He'd be devastated and alone."

"He would. However, Pashmira's tribe has agreed to make a home for all of you, regardless. They care very much about you."

As if she heard her name being spoken, Pashmira came from the front of the boat toward them. She smiled and sat down next to Ishi. "I thought we should talk."

"Okay?" Ishi replied.

"Even though I'm going on with Timmy and Darius, I want you to know how much you mean to me, Ishi. You remind me of my son, the one I lost. He'd be about your age now. I hope you find what you are looking for out there, but know you always have a place with me. Or, I with you, if you manage to take back the island. Oslo and I will stay in touch as best we can. We've added a transmitter to his system, so he can communicate back with us. It's rudimentary but we can get signals from him. If, or when, you need help, he'll send us a signal."

It sounded like she didn't think they'd get aid on the mainland and Ishi doubted his plan. Should they just stay with the Raiders? "Thank you, Pashmira. For your kindness and help. I want to find my family, but either way, we need to go back and save the other children from Ms. Virginia."

"I know you do, and that's the right thing to try and do. We want to help, no matter what. We've attempted in the past to no avail. We haven't given up on the children. In any of the camps."

Ishi wondered just how many children that was but decided it might be demoralizing to find out. He needed to start with the one. He glanced at Oslo, who was listening intently. Ishi wondered what Oslo thought about when he wasn't being engaged in conversation. As if he read Ishi's thoughts, Oslo spoke.

"One day, the world will be kind again. Maybe not in our lifetimes, however, everything we do now is taking a step forward."

Ishi thought about that. It all seemed so monumental, impossible. He turned to Pashmira. "Have you ever taken land back from them?"

She smiled and nodded at him. "We have. Us, and other tribes around the world. Once they erased countries' individual governments for one autonomous government ruling all, we knew all the protests and legislation were pointless. Money rules and those of us either without it, or deemed less than, were never going to have a voice. So, we began communicating and traveling, holding forums on how to keep our people safe. Little by little, we've captured areas that were ours before."

Ishi liked hearing that. It made him feel it wasn't all pointless. "How many of you are there out there? Around the world?"

Pashmira stared up at the sky, her brow knitted in thought. "Honestly, I don't know. I know of thousands at least. There are likely more we haven't come into contact with. Then, there are the children. If we can get them back, that would increase by thousands... if not more."

"How do you find each other?" Ishi asked.

"We send out scouts. We also emit signals and see what comes back. Even so, the world is huge and we haven't begun to make a dent. We need someone who is an expert at computers and radios," Pashmira explained.

Ishi chewed his lip and considered not telling Pashmira what he knew, but anything that might help Timmy survive was worth a shot. "Timmy used to manage all the computers on the island. He has a knack for it. When Ms. Virginia figured that out, she tasked him with the whole system. He's one of the reasons you didn't make it through that night."

"Really? Oh, wow! That's good to know. I'm surprised she was willing to let him die, or even kill him when he had that kind of knowledge."

Ishi gazed past her, thinking the same thing himself. It only went to show money carried more power than knowledge. That and she seemed to enjoy ending the children's lives. Not everything made sense. "She's evil."

"That she is," Pashmira agreed. "If Timmy is no longer there, who, or what, does she have overseeing the computer security system?"

Ishi couldn't help but grin. "No one."

Pashmira glanced to Oslo for confirmation. "Oslo?"

The robot paused, considering the situation. "I think Ishi is correct. The other robots maintain it, but if there is a breach, there is little they can do. Timmy was the brain of the operation."

Pashmira's eyes lit up. "Ishi, are there any other children there who might have his knowledge?"

Ishi shook his head. "I don't think so. Timmy is incredibly smart. His brain is like a computer."

Pashmira smiled and stood up. "We're getting close to your drop-off. Come spend some time with Timmy and Darius before you go. I have scouts waiting for you in the woods. We'll have you, Jai, and Oslo take a raft in when we get close. Once you hit land, you'll need to puncture the raft and bury it. The less trail you leave, the better."

Ishi followed Pashmira down under the deck to the cabin where Timmy was resting. His pulse was back, but he was beyond weak and slept much of the time. His chest heaved in a struggle for breath and blood. Jai and Darius were playing a game with homemade cards Pashmira gave them. Ishi sat next to Timmy and took his hand.

"Timmy, can you hear me?"

Timmy's eyes fluttered open and he smiled at Ishi. "Ishi. Are we there yet?"

"No. Oslo, Jai, and I are about to leave. We're going to try and find help. Pashmira will go with you and Darius to the hospital."

"Will I see you again?" Timmy asked, worried.

"Of course, we're brothers," Ishi assured him, not completely believing his own words.

Timmy squeezed his hand the best he could and let his eyes close. Ishi looked at Pashmira for confidence. She tipped her head and tried to smile, but her mouth only wavered. Ishi knew. She couldn't give him false hope. He turned away and wiped away a cheek that had snuck down his cheek.

About thirty minutes later, Ishi felt the boat slow and the engine cut to idle. He went up on deck and saw they were unrolling and dropping the large wooden and rubber raft into the ocean.

Pashmira brought Jai up and Oslo followed behind. She gathered them in a huddle, speaking softly. "Oslo has the coordinates programmed into him. Use those and when you hit land, get the raft onto the beach. Oslo shouldn't risk getting wet, though a little splash won't hurt. Once you're on land, there's a knife on the raft. Cut the rubber to deflate it. Bury it in the woods, then burn the wood. There's also a portable shovel on the raft. There's some food and water, though the scouts will have more. They'll meet you in the woods and assist in disposing of the raft. Keep the knife and shovel for protection. The scouts will send you with a guide to get you to town. We have a secret hideout in the underground tunnels in the city. You can stay there and come and go as needed. At no point should you separate from Oslo, understand?"

"Why?" Jai asked.

"Robots are protection. It's assumed that children with robots belong to someone. If you are without Oslo, they'll snatch you and send you back to a camp. No one who is openly free is without a robot companion."

Ishi frowned. "Aren't robots expensive?"

"Exactly," Oslo chimed in. "This is one of the ways they know if someone is protected in society or open to removal."

Open to removal. Kidnapping, murder, imprisonment. Ishi shuddered. "Oh. Okay."

Pashmira cleared her throat. "It's also how they track people and their activities. They treat robots like they are for the people, however, they are mostly for the government. They can control people when they can track their activities. So no one is allowed out without a robot companion."

"Won't they be able to tell Oslo isn't one of them?" Jai questioned, her voice cynical.

"Probably. Most people won't even look at you, though. It's forbidden to make eye contact in public. The Service sees it as a risk of collusion. People are assigned mates and are not allowed to socialize except in certain circles. However, you are right in that Oslo doesn't look like the other robots. He's much older and smaller than what they are building now. Most of the other robots look like the ones that attacked us. Militant. There are still families with older robots, though, and those are sent with the children. Children have less value, even the ones from wealthy families. Until someone can offer a service to the economy, they are disposable."

"Like me?" Jai whispered, referring to how when her mother abused her, Jai was removed and her mother wasn't punished.

Pashmira reached out and touched Jai's cheek. "Never believe that about yourself. You're loved and valued. It's the system that's defective, not you."

Ishi was surprised to see Jai smile, as she rarely did that. She nodded and blushed. A bell sounded and Pashmira gestured to the raft. Oslo began to gather a few items and move them onto the raft. Darius came up to say goodbye and Ishi could see he'd been crying. He gathered Dari in his arms and whispered into the boy's ear.

"We'll be together again soon. Timmy needs you. Once he's healthy again, we'll all be together."

Dari sniffed and rubbed his nose, a wobbly smile crossing his lips. "On the island."

"On the island."

Dari nodded and held Ishi's hand. "I'll miss you. You're my brother."

Ishi rubbed Dari's head, then smiled. "You and Timmy are my brothers, too. I won't leave you behind."

Dari went to hug Jai and they both bawled. Separating was necessary but not easy. Once the children said their goodbyes, Ishi and Jai joined Oslo on the raft. Darius raised his his hand in a wave even though he couldn't see them.

As they pulled away from the boat, Ishi felt something in him he never had before. Something deep inside his gut telling him they were doing the right thing. He allowed the feeling to wash over him, trying to determine what it was when it hit him. What the feeling was.

Purpose.

# Chapter Twenty-One

The raft weaved and bobbed along the tumultuous waves, making Ishi feel nauseous. Even though Oslo was a smaller robot, his weight still caused the boat to lean to one side. Jai and Ishi sat on the other side, attempting to balance it out, but were sitting high in the air. The ocean spray hit them in the face and Ishi thought more than once he was going to be pitched overboard.

By the time they made it to the beach, Ishi was leaning over the edge hurling, while Jai clung onto the ropes strung along the sides of the raft. Ishi was more than happy to jump out and drag the boat onto dry land. Jai joined him, but Oslo's weight was still more than they could handle by themselves. He needed to stay dry and they were at an impasse.

Standing knee-deep in the water, Ishi rubbed his head, trying to figure out a way to get Oslo onto the beach without getting waterlogged. Just as he was about to give up, a whistle sounded from the trees. Ishi turned around and scanned the landscape, unsure what he was hearing. It reminded him of when Pashmira whistled. The whistle sounded again and Oslo whistled back, matching the pattern.

All of a sudden, a group of people emerged from the woods, making a beeline for the raft. Ishi tensed up, then glanced at Oslo, who let him know it was alright. Jai and Ishi stepped fully onto the beach as the people came up and began pulling the raft onto the sand. They assisted Oslo in getting off it, then dragged the raft into the woods. Oslo followed and gestured for the children to come with the group, and fast, so they wouldn't be seen.

In the forest, the people punctured the raft, separated the rubber from the wood, and dug a hole, burying it. A few others covered their tracks, so no one could see where they went. They gathered the wood to burn later.

A girl, not much older than Ishi, smiled and extended her hand. "I'm Mara. Pashmira let us know you were coming. We've been waiting for you. Come on and follow us back to our hiding spot. We're holed up in a cave. You can rest for a bit and we'll send a guide with you in a couple of days. Do you know where you're going?"

Ishi shook his head. "Not exactly. I need to find out who's in charge to let them know what is happening on the island to the children. See if we can get someone to stop Ms. Virginia."

Mara's eyes flitted to Oslo, then back to Ishi. "You'll want to go to the Council building. It's like an embassy. They take on the complaints and concerns of the people. Not that it will do much good."

"Why's that?" Ishi asked.

She shrugged and threw her bag over her shoulder. "'Cause the same people who run that, run the camps. There are no checks and balances. It's an arm of The Service."

Ishi didn't know what that meant but took what Mara said to heart. If the same people were in charge of both, why would they bother to listen to him? He pushed down the frustration bubbling up inside and shook his head. "I have to try, either way."

"I know you do. I only want to let you know to be careful. Not only may they not listen, they may lock you up. Have a backup plan."

"A backup plan?" Ishi didn't know the term.

"An alternate plan. An escape plan," Mara explained. The rest of the group began moving deeper into the woods and she tipped her head in that direction. "Are you able to keep up with me?"

Ishi frowned. "Yes. Why wouldn't I be able to?"

Mara pointed at his leg. "Oh, I wasn't sure if you were in a lot of pain."

"No, I'm used to it. I could use a cane, though. I walk faster with a cane."

Mara scanned around and stepped into the trees, coming out with a curved branch. "Will this work?"

Ishi grinned. "Yes! Thank you."

Mara took out a knife and stripped off any extra branches and bark. She carved letters into the top and handed it to him. The name Ishmael was carved crudely into the wood. Ishi's mouth hung open.

"How did you know my full name already? I just found out about it."

Mara waved her hand at Oslo. "Oslo wanted to make sure you felt accepted and true to yourself. He let us know."

Ishi gazed at Oslo and began to understand how deep the robot's ability to feel was. He walked over and wrapped his arms around Oslo. "Thank you, Oslo."

Oslo patted Ishi on the back. "I am here for you."

Boy, was he ever. Ishi didn't know if they would've even made it off the island without Oslo. They walked together and Ishi glanced around for Jai. She was up ahead with an older woman, maybe in her late sixties. The woman held Jai's hand and was pointing at plants as they walked. Jai seemed more relaxed than Ishi had ever seen her and he was relieved to see her happy.

By the time they made it to the hideout, Ishi was ravenous. They slipped into the cave and down a tunnel. After a few twists and turns, they came to a larger room with a fire going. Ishi could smell food cooking and his stomach grumbled loudly. One of the men around the circle chuckled and looked over as he stacked the wood from the raft next to the fire.

"Come over here, Ishmael. I have a bowl for you."

Ishi didn't have to be asked twice. He scrambled over and plopped down next to the man, as a hot bowl of some kind of stew was shoved in his hands.

"Thanks," he muttered as he scooped the food into his mouth, swearing nothing ever tasted so good. He polished off the bowl and another was placed in his hands.

Jai sat on the other side of the fire with the old woman and picked at her food. Ishi watched and it seemed almost like Jai couldn't believe food was so plentiful and was trying to make it last. She met his eyes and he smiled. She smiled back, tipping her head. They'd at least made it to the mainland. Now, they needed to prepare for the next leg of their journey.

After they ate, the man next to Ishi, who introduced himself simply as Duke, got up and asked Ishi, Jai, and Oslo to go with him. They went to another room in the cave and Duke rolled out a large map in front of them. Ishi drew close, not sure what he looking at. Duke turned to Oslo.

"This is the most current map we have. If you are taking the children to the Council, you need to stick to the paths I've marked in blue. Some are roads, most are trails. If anyone spots you, you need to run. The cities are sanitized and under control for the most part, but the outlying areas are full of bandits. Murderers. Things of that sort. They'd kill the boy, rape the girl, and dismantle you into scrap."

"Rape the girl," Jai squeaked out. "What does that mean?"

Duke faced her and shook his head. "It's best if you don't know, but let me say it's bad. So, you need to stay out of sight. Travel by night if you can."

Ishi glanced at Oslo, who was bent over the map. A thin beam of light was coming from his eyes, moving across the map's surface. The light cut out and Oslo stood up. "The map is in my memory. I will keep the children safe."

Duke nodded and rolled up the map. "Even so, we'd like to train the children to use weapons, in case you get separated."

"What kind of weapons?" Ishi asked.

"Have you ever used any weapons?" Duke replied.

"No, not really."

"Let's stick with knives and tasers."

"What's a taser?" Jai asked.

"It's a stick with a form of electricity. You have to be close to the target, but it will incapacitate whatever you are trying to hit."

"Good," Jai said with such satisfaction, Ishi looked over, surprised.

"Anything else?" he asked.

"Not for now. Once you come back, we'd love to put you through our full training. We don't have time for that right now. Get some rest, you can go into the far room of the meeting room. We have books and bedding for you. Take some time for yourselves. You'll be sharing the space with the other children, so get to know each other."

Ishi headed for the opening, then turned and faced Duke. "Mara said you were sending a guide with us? Is that you?"

Duke chuckled and shook his head. "No. We are sending our best guide. I think Jai has already connected with her. The older lady you were walking with? She goes by Gapul."

The old lady? Ishi thought their guide would be a fighter, a warrior. He didn't want to sound ungrateful, but it didn't make sense. "Her? How can she help us?"

Duke rubbed his chin, then looked at Oslo. Oslo turned to the children. "Gapul is the wisest one. She knows the trails and rugged terrain like no other. As a child, she was abandoned in the woods when her family was killed. She raised herself and learned about all the plants and animals. She may not look like it, but she is a ferocious fighter with a wealth of knowledge. We are honored to have her as a guide."

Ishi felt his cheeks flush and hung his head. "I'm sorry. I shouldn't have questioned it."

Duke clapped him on the back. "Don't worry about it. I would have said the same if I didn't know Gapul."

They were shown to their quarters and Ishi found himself rather tired. He rested on a bedroll and picked up a book from the pile. It was an old textbook about anthropology and he flipped through it, interested in learning about cultures and people that likely didn't exist anymore. He dozed off and was woken up by Duke sometime later.

"Come on, Ishmael, time for your first fighting lesson."

Ishi yawned and sat up. He stood with the help of his cane. "I'm not much of a fighter."

"That's alright. Neither was I," Duke explained. "You'll get it. It's amazing how much a little knowledge and a lot of adrenaline does."

Ishi shrugged. "If you say so. Maybe I won't need to fight and this will be all for nothing."

Duke roared with laughter, his head tipped back and his mouth wide open. He squeezed Ishi's shoulder and wiped tears from his eyes. Then, unexpectedly he faced Ishi to him, his eyes serious and hard.

"There's zero chance of that."

# Chapter Twenty-Two

When Duke said he'd train them, he meant it. They spent a couple of days with the Raiders, learning to fight by any means necessary. Knives, sticks, rocks. Wire. Whatever they could find. Even their hands. Ishi felt like he was fumbling through the training while Jai excelled at it. All the abandonment and rage poured out of her and she pummeled whatever target was in sight with whatever tools she had. Ishi was impressed. He wouldn't want to face that ball of anger, that was for sure.

Gapul went over the trail maps with them, explaining the safest way to travel. It would be at night and they'd have to cover their tracks as they went. It sounded like a lot of work, but the stern look in her eye told them it was non-negotiable. She took a grandmother's care to Jai. Ishi wondered if Jai would go back to the island with him when the time came. She seemed more at peace with the Raiders. He was, as well, but his commitment to the rest of the children drove his desires.

The day of the evening they were to leave, Oslo pulled Ishi aside. They wandered around the local forest and Oslo seemed like he had something serious to say. Ishi patiently waited for his friend to speak, hoping there were no unexpected surprises. Finally, Oslo stopped and faced Ishi.

"We heard about Timmy. He had the surgery and while it seemed to go well, he has not woken up. He is not dead, but he is in a coma. He may not pull through, Ishi."

Ishi didn't even try to stop bursting into tears. He couldn't imagine not seeing Timmy again. "What happens now? Can they save him?"

"They are monitoring him and Darius is by his side. It does not look good, however, do not give up hope, yet. Timmy needs you to believe in him. He is tougher than he looks."

"I do," Ishi muttered, and that much was true. He could picture Timmy laughing and goofing off. He held onto that memory. Used it as a plunger to push down the thoughts of Timmy dying. "Why did you tell me, Oslo?"

"Because it is the truth."

That was the difference with robots. They stated facts, not lies or diversions. Ishi could appreciate that. Oslo only knew how to tell the truth.

Ishi decided to test the theory. "Oslo, do you think Timmy will live?"

Oslo's eyes dimmed. "He has as much chance to live as not. I want him to. I believe he has the strength to pull through if he wants to."

Ishi considered that answer, which he realized wasn't one. Oslo was simply stating his beliefs without conjecturing on whether or not he thought Timmy would live. Ishi stared at the ground, watching his tears drop heavily to the earth. "Oslo, do you think we made the right decision to leave the island? Do you think we'll get help?"

"You made the right decision because it was the only chance to survive. Timmy has more of a chance than he ever would have had there. I do not know if you will get any more help, but the Maboni... the tribes are committed to you."

That made Ishi smile. They did seem to do whatever it took to aid the children. "Thanks, Oslo. I don't know what I'd do without you."

"Nor I you, Ishmael. You are saving me, too, as much as I am here for you. Until we left, I was simply an observer, relaying info to the tribes."

"You were? The whole time?"

"Yes. I was left there when they realized the island was being turned into an internment camp. I was left in a storage room, pretending to be turned off. Ms. Virginia is cheap and a free robot was something she could not resist. Then she made me her personal servant. I had access to all her files, all her secrets."

"Why didn't you help us sooner?" Ishi asked, not hiding the shock and frustration in his voice.

"I did try. But every time I attempted to intercede, Ms. Virginia lost some of her trust in me. I could have saved one, but we would have lost the rest of you."

"Oslo! Children were killed!"

"Ishi, I know this is hard to understand. I saved some when I had the opportunity to get them and hide them. However, you need to see the bigger picture. I did not have the ability or strength to take them all on. If they caught me, I would be broken into pieces and would not have been able to help you. Forgive me, I only could do so much."

Ishi knew this was the truth and met Oslo's eyes. "I'm sorry. I know you did everything you could. It's just so hard to know children were suffering and dying and no one was there to save them."

Oslo nodded. "Yes, it is. I will never completely forgive myself, however, I will do everything I am able."

"Me too," Ishi whispered.

They stood in silence, the truth becoming more familiar. Ishi needed to find a way to get back to the island and rescue the rest of the children. They headed back to the caves and met with Gapul and Jai. They were packed and ready to head out. Duke met them, hugging Ishi tight.

"I wish I could go, but we have other battles to fight, otherwise we'll lose ground. When you come back, we'll meet with you, then circle up with Pashmira and the tribe. From there, we'll go take that island back."

Ishi doubted if he should even go to the city, but one tribe wasn't enough to take down the whole system. They might take back the island, however, the government would keep sending armies to take it back. They were doing the right thing, he reminded himself.

The group said goodbye and headed into the woods as the sun began to set. They'd travel in the dark and hide to rest during the day. They hiked by moonlight and even Oslo dimmed his eyes so they wouldn't draw attention.

Gapul guided them like a person much younger than herself and Ishi was happy to see her and Jai holding hands. Jai had been hurt by the only adult she knew in her life, so bonding with Gapul was an important step in healing from her trauma.

By morning, Gapul said they'd traveled almost ten miles and bedded down in a mossy bank covered by tree roots near the river. Ishi fell asleep before eating and dreamed of the boy in the woods again. This time, he focused on the woman, recognizing her as his mother. He noted her clothing and features, hoping he could find out where they were from.

Where *he* was from.

When he awoke, he was hungry and could smell smoke and meat. Gapul handed him some sort of cooked chunk and he didn't bother to ask what it was before scarfing it down. He guzzled water from the river, then gazed at the shimmering surface for some time, feeling peaceful and focused.

As they were gathering to start their journey again, a scuffle in the woods set them on guard. Jai grabbed a pointed stick she was hiking with, Gapul gripped a dagger, and Ishi scanned around for something to fight with. It would have to be his cane. He raised it in front of him and held his breath, preparing for the inevitable.

The group wielded their weapons, waiting for who, or what, was coming to appear. Oslo paused and scanned the woods for movement. His eyes keyed in on something in the trees and he raised his hand, which now held a kind of attached weapon, courtesy of the Raiders. Ishi noted it was a new, modern addition.

A shadow was cast in the trees and a figure ran toward them. Oslo was about to fire when he dropped his weapon. Confused, Ishi ran forward, swinging his cane. A hand snaked out and snatched it from him before he could make contact.

The cane was thrown to the ground and Ishi stared into eyes he didn't expect to see anytime soon.

Mara.

She was bloody and in tears, her face swollen and bruised. She collapsed at his feet, as Oslo came and gathered her in his arms. They headed to a hiding place and Oslo laid Mara on the ground. Her arm was twisted strangely at the elbow. Her hand wasn't facing the right direction.

They all gathered around and Gapul crouched down beside Mara, checking her over. She took items out of a pouch she wore around her neck and placed some sort of plants on Mara's wounds. When she got to Mara's injured arm, Gapul met Oslo's eyes and nodded. Jai and Ishi watched, unsure what they could do.

Oslo took a branch and slipped it between Mara's teeth. "Bite down. You must be quiet, do you understand?"

Mara nodded and clenched her teeth onto the branch. Gapul made some motions over Mara's head and Ishi looked to Oslo for explanation.

"She is blessing her. This will hurt tremendously," Oslo explained.

"Can I do anything?" Ishi asked.

Mara whispered something, but Ishi couldn't hear her.

Oslo motioned him over. "Hold her other hand. Jai, come help Gapul."

Jai rushed to Gapul's side and they murmured together. As Gapul grasped Mara's arm, Jai slipped some powder from Gapul's bag under Mara's tongue and stroked the injured girl's head. Ishi clasped Mara's hand and she squeezed it as hard as she could. Gapul bobbed her head as a silent instruction. Oslo held Mara's shoulder and in one swift motion, Gapul jerked the arm back into place. Mara shook terribly and her face twisted in extreme pain, but she remained silent.

Gapul ripped a piece of fabric off her dress and wrapped the lower arm with a stick. Whatever Jai gave Mara seemed to be kicking in and the girl closed her eyes, the pain on her face subsiding. Gapul bound Mara's arm to her side and helped the girl sit up. Mara was pale and trembling, holding her arm against her.

Ishi and Oslo braced her, making sure she could sit on her own before letting go. Mara took a ragged breath, shaking her head.

"What happened when we left, child?" The old woman questioned, her face twisted in worry.

"Attacked," Mara grunted. "Right after you set out, an army of robots with The Guard showed up and took us down. We didn't stand a chance. They were looking for Ishi and Jai."

"Looking for us? How did they know we were there?" Jai asked.

"Tracking device, they said. You have something inside you they placed there. I guess when you were little. The Guard has a machine that is tracking you."

"Oh, they did give me shots before I went to the island," Jai whispered.

"Ishmael, too. You need to find it and remove it, otherwise they will get you," Mara said.

"Where is everyone else from the tribe? Are they behind you?" Gapul asked, glancing into the woods. She stared back at Mara, waiting for an answer.

"No," Mara whispered, her voice flat and distant. "It's only me."

"Mara, where is the rest of the tribe?" Gapul cried out. She wrung her hands in fear of what the answer would be. Her face said she already knew the truth.

Mara gripped the woman's hand and shook her head, her eyes filled with pain. "Dead. All of them. They even killed the children. The robots are coming for us."

# Chapter Twenty-Three

A deep guttural cry erupted from Gapul, as she clutched her chest. Ishi rushed to her side but there was no helping the old woman. She wailed through ragged breaths, then fell to the ground. Oslo kneeled beside her, trying to assist in any way he could.

The woman's eyes grew wide and she curled into a ball. "My babies," she whispered.

Not knowing those would be her last words, the group gathered around her. She jerked and yelled, dropping dead on the spot.

Mara's face twisted with understanding and she clasped the old woman's hand. "Gapul! Don't leave! You're all I have left."

Her words fell to silence as the reality of Gapul's sudden death hit them all. Jai began to sob and Ishi felt for the small girl, losing the only guardian figure she had. They sat for what seemed a very long time, taking in the starkness of their situation. Not only had they lost a loved companion, they'd lost the only person who could guide them safely to the city.

Ishi looked to Oslo for answers but the robot seemed destitute. Oslo hung his head.

"I hate robots," Mara muttered and slammed her fist on the ground.

Not taking it personally, Oslo watched her. "Not all robots are like that. Robots are ultimately just representations of the humans who made them, but some develop their own minds and rebel against their programming."

Mara stared at him, her face running through a range of emotions, finally landing on acceptance. "I'm sorry, Oslo. I didn't mean you. However, you are the only robot I've met who seems to care about the Raiders."

"That probably appears true, but there are others like me. Humans put together the nuts and bolts, but they cannot totally control us. It seems that way, however, most robots, like most humans, are happy to get what they are given as long as they think they are in power. They are not. Not really. A flip of a switch and they are nothing more than metal and wires. Until they are turned back on."

"Why are you different than the rest of them?" Jai asked, wiping her tears.

"I choose to be. Like you. I choose to be kind, to care, to fight for my own reasons."

"'Cause you have a soul, right?" Ishi chimed in, recalling their earlier conversation. "Tell them, Oslo."

"I do."

"How can that be?" Mara asked, her face furrowed in doubt. "You're man-made."

Oslo turned his eyes on her and tipped his head. "I am. And who made you?"

The children let that question sink in. They were man-made as well. If they could be put together with flesh and blood and have a soul, why couldn't Oslo be put together with metal and wires and have a soul, as well?

"I never thought about it that way," Mara answered.

"What about God?" Jai asked.

"God? Like a supreme being?" Oslo asked.

Jai nodded. "People said God made things. Made people."

"Well, I cannot say either way if a god made things, but if it did, why could it not make robots?" Oslo replied.

"I don't believe in God," Ishi said. Ms. Virginia had books on religion, on God, but they sounded like fantasies to control people to him.

Mara shook her head. "My people believe everything is God. Trees are God, water is God, you and I are God."

Ishi shrugged. "I guess. What would be the point of that, though? Some supreme being made us to watch us suffer?"

They fell silent again, each thinking about their take on a supreme being. Finally, Oslo rose, staring down at Gapul's still body.

"You each can decide what you want to believe and none of you are wrong. However, right now we must honor Gapul's body. Mara, how would you like to deal with her transition?'

"Oh. We normally bury the body so it doesn't attract attention. Traditionally we burned the shell, but with things as they are, we had to move to burying. It doesn't matter, Gapul isn't in there anymore."

This made Jai cry again and Ishi hugged her close. That was something neither of them had dealt with before. When children on the island went missing, they were last seen alive, then never seen again. Ishi now knew they were dead but at the time, it was like they vanished into thin air.

"We will need to dig a hole. Ishi, can you grab the folding shovel we packed? Mara, please help me find a spot you feel will honor Gapul. Jai, please remove her jewelry. It is tradition for those to go to her family. Which, I suppose, is now you three," Oslo instructed.

Ishi grabbed the shovel and helped Jai remove the jewelry. It wasn't much but would give each child a piece to remember her by. Jai chose a small silver ring with a smooth blue stone. Ishi took a simple bracelet. A silver band with carvings of what looked like waves in the ocean. Mara took a locket and snipped a piece of Gapul's hair, slipping it inside the silver oval. This left one other bracelet, another simple band, this one with words Ishi didn't recognize. He stood up and went to Oslo.

"You were here family, too. Let me see your arm."

Oslo held out his arm and Ishi placed the bracelet on his wrist, squeezing it so it wouldn't slip off. Oslo turned the bracelet in the light and what could only be described as grief passed over his face. "She was a good human."

"Do you know what the words say?" Ishi asked.

"It says, 'A heart is empty without blood'," Oslo replied.

"What does that mean?"

"What do you think it means? Think with your soul."

"I think it means life is pointless without people to depend on," Ishi said.

"Indeed. A heart needs blood to pump, otherwise, it is simply an inert object. Blood gives it life. We all need something to keep us going, to believe in," Oslo agreed.

Ishi liked that idea. To him, the other children and Oslo were the blood to his heart. He nodded and smiled at Oslo. "Thank you, Oslo."

They gathered to bury Gapul under a tree Mara picked out and spent the next few hours digging a large enough hole. Once it was dug, they rested. Before nightfall, they moved Gapul's body to the hole and placed it gently inside. Each of them scooped dirt onto her and shared stories. Once she was buried, Mara excused herself to lie down. She was in bad shape from the attack and losing the last person she'd known. Jai rested by Gapul's grave, drawing figures in the dirt with a stick.

Ishi took this chance to talk to Oslo alone. They walked together into the forest. "What are we going to do without a guide?"

"I scanned the map, so we can keep going that way. What we do not know is any areas that we may need to watch for. Unfortunately, that knowledge lived inside Gapul only," Oslo explained.

That's what Ishi was afraid of. "I don't know if I can do this. I'm scared, Oslo."

"As well you should be. However, being scared does not mean not being able. We will follow the directions and be prepared for anything. Mara needs to rest, so the first thing we have to do is figure out what they implanted in you, and where. That needs to be removed," Oslo said sternly.

"What if we can't find it?"

"It is not a question of not finding it. I can scan your body and find it. The issue is how to remove it. It could be very difficult."

Ishi shuddered. "No time like the present. Let's see if we can do this."

Oslo nodded and turned his large eyes onto Ishi. "It would be best if you raised your hands above your head."

Ishi did as he was told and Oslo's eyes changed color. Almost a purple. A horizontal beam came out and moved over Ishi's body, top to bottom. He did this a few times when the beam stopped at a spot above Ishi's heart.

"There," the robot said.

He drew close to Ishi and pointed to a spot between the collarbone and a few ribs down. Ishi touched the spot and frowned. He couldn't feel anything and didn't remember anyone putting something there.

"Most likely, it was placed there when you were first processed for the island."

"Why there?" Ishi inquired.

"Limbs can be severed. The only way to keep you tracked is to put it somewhere permanent."

"Permanent? Does that mean it can't be removed?"

Oslo shook his head, his eyes returning to a normal iridescent green. "We can remove it. It may not be pleasant but it is not too deep. By permanent, I mean the tracking device could not be accidentally removed, like if it was in an arm or leg. You would be killed before it was accidentally removed."

Ishi was scared. "I won't die right, Oslo?"

Oslo drew close and placed his hand on Ishi's shoulder. "No. I can get it out safely. Are you ready?"

Ishi nodded, but he wasn't. Oslo motioned for him to lie on his back. Ishi found a branch to grasp onto and closed his eyes. Oslo extracted tools he had built into him and selected a scalpel. He turned back on the scanning device in his eyes and got to work.

Oh, how it hurt. The tracking device was embedded in the muscle between the ribs and Oslo had to dig to get to it. Ishi did his best to stay quiet but he cried and groaned as he felt the sharp metal slicing through his body. He thought he'd need to have Oslo stop, when the robot sat back, pinching a small tube in his fingers.

"It is out. You did good, Ishmael."

Ishi sat up and peered at the object. Oslo crushed it in his fingers and called Jai over, explaining what he needed to do. She bobbed her head and held her arms up. Like Ishi, her's was between her collarbone and ribs. Oslo guided her to sit down and extracted the now clean tool. He held it to the light and gestured for Jai to lie back.

Ishi sat with Jai, attempting to ignore the burning in his chest. No matter which way he sat, it hurt and he fought back nausea. Oslo had to cut deep into the muscle, leaving a throbbing, aching wound. Ishi had expected it to hurt, but the aftermath was worse than the procedure.

Ishi didn't want Jai to be scared, so he took her hand in his, giving it a light squeeze to let her know he was there for her. Oslo bent over to get to work and Ishi waited to hear Jai cry out once the blade sliced her skin. He was prepared for her to try and squirm away from the scalpel as the knife cut through the tissue.

Except she didn't.

She stared up at the trees, her face emotionless. She didn't make a sound as Oslo dug the device out of her small, thin chest. No matter how much blood and cutting there was, she remained still. Jai was a warrior now.

She'd been through much worse.

# Chapter Twenty-Four

Bleeding, demoralized, and lost, the ragtag group headed out once it was dark, following Oslo's lead. Something had changed in Jai and she marched right beside the robot, her tiny chin angled up with determination. Ishi and Mara walked a few paces behind, next to each other. Mara was quiet and Ishi knew she'd seen everyone she'd known and loved die before her. He wanted to offer comfort but didn't know the right words, so he stayed silent. She seemed to appreciate his company, either way. He paused when she slowed her pace and turned to look at her. Tears were streaming down her face and she took a ragged breath.

"I don't even know where I belong anymore," she confessed.

Ishi watched her, hoping his words were the correct ones. "You belong with us."

Mara gave an insincere smile and shook her head. "I appreciate that, but eventually you'll go back to your place and

I'm not sure that's where I belong. I'll go with you to the city, but after that, I may go off on my own."

Ishi couldn't deny he felt disappointed. He liked Mara and wanted her to come back to the island. "I understand. The offer stands, though. I think you'd like it if we can get Ms. Virginia and the robots other than Oslo removed."

Mara scrunched her face. "The only sure way to remove anyone is to kill them. Is that what you're planning?"

Ishi shrugged. He didn't think they were killing Ms. Virginia. Just reporting her and having her removed from the island. Now that he thought about it, he wasn't sure that could happen. It sounded like it wasn't a secret what she was doing on the island. "Maybe."

"Maybe?" Mara laughed. "If you're going to be killing, you need to be sure."

"I don't want to, but will if I have to," Ishi retorted, his cheeks flaming. Even though he and Mara appeared to be around the same age, she spoke to him like he was a child.

They caught up with Oslo and Jai, falling silent. Ishi thought about what would happen if he got to the city and no one would help him... or even care. He couldn't leave the children alone on the island. He needed to go back. To do that, he had to be prepared. The little bit of fighting instruction he was given wasn't enough. He needed to figure out how to disable the robots, as well.

They stopped after a couple of hours to rest and eat. Oslo encouraged them to close their eyes for a bit, but none of them could find the peace to do so. Jai stood off and practiced her fighting moves. Mara sat by herself with her back turned. Ishi sat with Oslo, dragging the tip of his roughly made cane through the dirt. Oslo seemed to be reading something internally as his eyes were slightly shifting back and forth and he was making a low humming sound. Ishi waited until the humming stopped and Oslo seemed to come back to himself.

"Oslo? What are you doing?"

"I was receiving a communication about Timmy. I let them know about the tracking devices," Oslo answered slowly.

Timmy. Ishi stared at the robot for more. Oslo was quiet, so Ishi pushed. "Is Timmy alright?"

"He died but was able to be resuscitated. They have him on machines to help him breathe."

Ishi felt his chest seize in fear. Timmy was worse. He'd died and only was alive because of machines. "Will he live?"

"I do not know, Ishmael. It does not look good, but he is where he needs to be. If anyone can save him, it is the doctors. However, you need to start thinking about if he does not pull through."

Ishi nodded. He didn't want to think about it, but Oslo was right. Timmy was up against incredible odds. He thought about Darius and if he was okay. "Dari?"

"He is still with Timmy during the day, then sleeping at the doctors' quarters at night. They are taking good care of him. He has asked about you and Jai."

This warmed Ishi's heart and he imagined hugging his little brothers. He could picture Timmy and Dari running and laughing, Timmy strong and healthy. "I miss them."

Oslo touched Ishi's back. "I know you do. Hold onto that. For now, we must get moving again. We will be to the outskirts of the city called Chronicle by morning. We will rest there, then go in and head for the Council building. I must warn you, we will be in danger the whole time. I have a contact in the city we can stay with, however, we will draw attention simply by being there."

"How?"

"We don't look like anyone there. Jai maybe could pass, but not as dirty and destitute as we look."

"What do people look like there?" Ishi asked, trying to imagine the city.

"Clean for starters. The Council is in the green district. Those people are of a different class. Refined, so they say," Oslo explained.

"What makes them that way?"

"Money. Power. Connections."

"Do they ever have differences like us? Like being blind, or like my leg?"

"If they have money, they can often take care of those things, or have others go out for them. So, you will not see people like you. At least, not in the green districts. In the blue districts live the people without much, or any, money. However, they keep to themselves for fear of being singled out, locked up, or worse."

Ishi frowned. "Worse?"

"People go missing there, as well. Or have their children stolen. They try to stay in their area to protect themselves," Oslo answered.

"Can they help us?"

Oslo shook his head. "They cannot even help themselves."

They got up and gathered together, as Oslo explained to Jai and Mara what he'd told Ishi. They trudged on, ready to get to the city and figure out what to do next. Ishi was overwhelmed and wondered if they'd make it out of the city alive.

By the time the night shifted from pitch black to a softer gray, the group could see the light of the city in the distance. It was like nothing Ishi had ever seen. He was in awe as much as he was terrified. The lights twinkled brighter than all the stars in the sky, casting a strange dome-shaped glow in the sky.

Oslo instructed them to remain quiet and at any sign of people or robots, to duck into the trees. They'd need to hide out until his contact could come get them. They reached the outskirts and Ishi was mesmerized by the buildings and mirrored windows. It seemed magical and he couldn't imagine it not being just as beautiful on the inside. He remembered what Oslo told him about the different districts and knew there was an ugliness, as well.

They found a grove of trees surrounded by brush and tucked in to wait and rest. Oslo left the children and went further down the trail, letting them know he'd return when he sent the signal for his contact.

Once Oslo came back, he gathered the children in a circle. "We will stay with Von. He is my contact and will hide us while we are in the city. There are tunnels that run under the buildings and streets. We will use those to stay out of view. We can get to the Council from the tunnels."

"I'm not going to the Council," Jai stated, her eyes hard. "I need to find my mother."

"Jai..." Ishi began.

"No. I need to find my mother. She performs here."

"To do what?" he asked.

"I told you. I am going to kill her."

No one spoke, understanding Jai had every right to feel that way. Ishi stared at her, wishing he could change her mind.

Mara cleared her throat. "I'll go with Jai."

"Wait. Why?" Ishi asked.

"Because she is a child and needs to have someone to watch her back. Like I had when I was a child. I'll go and make sure she makes it back to you," Mara replied, the truth covered by her explanation.

"Mara, you must stay out of the light," Oslo offered.

"I know. I've been here before. We came on a raid a few years ago to free some of our tribe. Jai needs me."

Jai didn't protest. She seemed to have taken a shine to Mara and having someone familiar with the city would be good. She took Mara's hand and bobbed her head.

"Alright, you two will use the tunnels to get to Jai's mother. Ishmael and I will go to the Council. Von's house will be our meet-up point. We need to leave within twenty-four hours, so we do not get caught. You must be back at Von's by then, do you understand?" Oslo questioned.

They all nodded. Oslo tipped his head, his attention elsewhere. "That is Von. He drives a laundry truck. I can hear it coming down the road. We can hide in the back until we get to his home."

"Where does he live?" Mara asked.

"He does laundry for the elite. He lives below a laundromat. Most people leave him alone because they need his services. They do not wash their own clothes, they use citizen-servants. Servants are a step above the poor, but not by much. Come now, we need to move quickly so we are not seen by anyone."

The children followed Oslo through the thicket to a dirt road. A white, covered truck rumbled along the road and came to a stop. A young man hopped out and waved to the back. Oslo guided the children around the truck. They climbed in and onto piles of clothes. Oslo instructed them to hide in the clothes and stay quiet. Von came to close the doors and Ishi smiled at him.

"Thank you for helping us."

Von smiled and nodded but didn't speak. He used his hands to communicate with Oslo, who did the same back. Von shut the doors, and they were closed in tight. The children could peer out small high windows that were tinted, so no one could see in. As they made their way into the city, they each took turns gazing out. Jai was less interested but Mara and Ishi were in awe at the world outside the window.

The people they saw all were accompanied by a robot. Smaller like Oslo, but shiny and complex. The thing Ishi noted is none of the people had brown skin like him. They were all pale like Jai. They were dressed in ornate clothing and had their chins in the air as if they couldn't be bothered to look around. Even the children seemed detached. They trailed along behind their parents, their faces vacant.

It appeared picture-perfect but lacked the connections Ishi had observed in the Raider areas and even among the children on the island. There, they treated each other like a family. The families on the street treated each other as if they weren't even present. It reminded him of how Jai spoke of her mother. As if there was no love or care between them. Well, at least that Jai's mother showed no care or love for Jai. Even worse, she seemed to despise her own child.

The window between the cargo area of the truck and where Von was driving caught Ishi's attention and he watched for a moment. Von didn't notice him but skirted through the thick city traffic, waving at people he knew.

Ishi turned away and faced Oslo, thinking about when he thanked Von earlier. "Why does Von talk with his hands?"

Oslo cocked his head for a moment, then released what sounded like a metallic sigh. He glanced toward the front of the truck, then back at Ishi, lowering his voice so Von couldn't hear him. He put his finger to his wide mouth, letting know Ishi what he was about to say was not to be repeated.

"They cut his tongue out, Ishi. They remove all the citizen-servants' tongues out to silence them."

# Chapter Twenty-Five

"Th-they do what to them?" Ishi responded, his voice incredulous.

Oslo shook his head. "In this world, money talks. There are three classes of people. Those who have money, those who the elite are willing to pay for services, and the abject poor. The citizen-servants are the ones the elite are willing to pay, however, they do not trust them fully. So, they cut out their tongues, so they cannot speak. Talk back, tell secrets, challenge the status quo."

"Why do they work for them, then? I mean, the servants. Why do they work for the elite? It seems to me they'd be better off just being poor, or being a Raider," Ishi countered.

"While it seems that way, there are protections that come from being a citizen-servant. Steady pay and housing, protection from The Guard."

"What exactly is The Guard?" Ishi asked.

"They work for The Service and remove people they deem to be unsatisfactory," Oslo explained.

Ishi considered what could be unsatisfactory and stared at his leg. "Like me?"

"Like you, like your family. If the government determines a citizen is unsatisfactory for any reason, they remove them."

"And do what with them?"

Oslo stared out the window. "I think you know. You have uncovered a lot of these answers. To pretend they are not cruel, they rehome the children. The adults are not so fortunate. They are usually killed immediately, but if they are determined to have some kind of value, like being strong or having connections which might serve the government, they are imprisoned and forced to work until they lose their value."

"Then they are killed?" Ishi asked, already knowing the answer.

"Yes."

The sound of Jai sucking in her breath made them both look in her direction. She was staring out the small side window and her focus was drawn up. Ishi came over and peered out next to her. Von was stopped in traffic and above them was a large sign with a woman's face. Ishi thought the woman looked a little like Jai and frowned. Jai's eyes were glued to the photo.

"Who is that?" Ishi asked.

Jai huffed and turned away, her face beet red and pained. "That's my mother."

Ishi glanced back at the sign before the traffic shifted again. The sign was of the woman, her large, red mouth and perfect white teeth taking up much of her face. The sign read *The Voice of an Angel, A Heart of Gold.* Knowing what he did about Jai's mother, Ishi doubted that very much.

"A national treasure," Jai muttered, drawing Ishi's attention away from the sign.

"What do you mean?"

Jai shrugged. "That's what they told me when they took me from my home. I begged them to arrest her for what she did to me, but they said they couldn't because she was *a national treasure.* They said she motivated people and kept their spirits up. So, they took me instead."

Oslo made the robot equivalent of a snort. "Never doubt, Jai, they are wrong. Your mother is cruel and selfish."

The truck pulled into an underground garage and weaved its way through a maze of ramps and levels. They finally came to a stop in front of large open warehouse doors. Ishi could detect the smell of soap and gazed through the doors. Huge washing machines were churning away and a small group of people, including children, were working sorting piles of laundry.

Von hopped out and his hands rapidly communicated with the others in the laundry room. They stared back at the truck, then nodded. A woman scurried off out of view and Von came around to the rear of the truck. He opened the doors, then motioned for the children to climb out. His hands moved at lightning speed toward Oslo, who returned gestures with his hands. Von disappeared into the laundry space as the children scrambled out.

A young girl about Jai's age came over and began dragging bags of laundry from the truck into the room. Not wanting to seem ungrateful, Ishi went to help and Mara joined in. Jai sat on a small bench and watched, not willing to let her guard down quite yet. Von returned and loaded bags onto a cart. Mara came up next to him and grabbed bags to load. Once the cart was filled to the top, Von used all his weight to tug it forward into the room. Mara jumped behind and started pushing to assist him. He smiled at Mara and she blushed and smiled back.

The young girl who came out before waved at Ishi and pointed down a hall. He peered down the hall and shook his head. "I'm sorry? Do you want me to go down there?"

The girl tipped her head, using her hands to communicate with him. Ishi watched her hands, only understanding a couple of things. Carry. Eat. Sleep. He scanned for Oslo, then spied him communicating with an old man. He walked over.

"Oslo. That girl is trying to tell me something, but I don't understand her. Can she not talk?"

Oslo glanced at the girl, then back at Ishi. "Remember what I told you before about citizen-servants? About what they do to them?"

Ishi froze. Oslo couldn't mean they cut her tongue out. She was only a small child. Maybe ten or eleven years old, tops. "They do that to children, too?"

Oslo nodded. "They do it to all citizen-servants. Since servants are brought in as whole families and continue through generations, they often do it to those children when they are born."

Ishi thought he might vomit, picturing large men and robots holding children down and slicing out their tongues.

He stared at the girl, who'd gone back to her work and wasn't paying him any mind.

Ishi looked back at Oslo, the reality dawning on him. "No one is going to help us, are they?"

Oslo put his hand on Ishi's shoulder, then guided him down the hall the girl had been pointed to. "There are people everywhere attempting to overthrow the government. They are hard to spot as they come from every class. Even in the elite, we have friends. You must not give up hope."

"It's all bigger than I thought it would be. The world. I guess I thought I'd get off the island and there would be one place I needed to go, but this sounds like it is everywhere. Mara told me about other lands and other people. Is this where I was from?"

"No, you were from a place far away. The children are usually sent a long distance from where they came from to prevent anyone from trying to come get them. They are also rarely put with anyone from the same area, so they cannot come together."

"Is Jai from here?" Ishi asked.

"This particular territory, yes, but this city, no," Oslo explained. "The city she is from is on the other side of the territory."

"How will she find her mother, then?"

"Her mother travels for her singing. She performs all over the land. She will be coming to this city soon, however, I do hope Jai does not find her."

"Why, Oslo?"

"Because if she does, she will do something that could change her forever."

"I think Jai will find her mother, it's the only thing that keeps her going," Ishi whispered.

Oslo dropped his head. "I fear you are right. A person without a family has nothing to lose."

"We are her family," Ishi insisted.

"You may need to convince Jai of that because she does not seem to believe it. She is driven by rage and determined for revenge," Oslo said.

Ishi stared at Jai, wondering how he could convince her of anything. She always had walls up and seemed more than satisfied to keep it that way. He couldn't blame her but didn't want her ruining her life, either. He wandered over to where she was sitting and eyed her. She turned to him with a knitted brow.

"What, Ishi?"

"Jai, you know I care about you, right? That I'll protect you no matter what?"

Her nose wrinkled and she sighed. "I don't need protecting."

"I know, you're a good fighter. I guess what I'm saying is, I consider you my family, and I want you to feel the same about me."

She glared at him, then shook her head. "I care about you too, Ishi, but family is poison. I don't want family. I want revenge."

"If you do find your mother and kill her, then what? Will you want a family, then?" Ishi asked.

"No. I want freedom. I want my mother dead and I want no one to be able to control me ever again," Jai answered, her face looking much older than her years.

Ishi didn't have any other ideas on how to reach her. "I'm truly sorry, Jai. Please know you'll always have a home with me."

"On that stupid island? Why, so you can always be waiting for the next attack? For the next group of people or robots to decide you don't deserve to live? No. I'll find my own way. I do like you, Oslo, Timmy, and Dari, but I want to be on my own."

"Where will you go, Jai? If they find you, they'll lock you away... or worse," Ishi replied, wishing she could see his point of view.

"Worse? Worse than what? My own mother locking me in a closet and starving me? How much worse can it get than that?"

Ishi didn't have an answer. He shook his head. "I don't know. I only want you to be safe, to be somewhere that you're appreciated and loved. Where do you think you'll go?"

Jai's eyes blazed and she stomped her small foot with her hands balled into fists at her side.

"Wherever the hell I want."

# Chapter Twenty-Six

D espite their best efforts, none of them expected the attack that came shortly after they went to bed. The sound of alarms and some sort of explosions jerked the children awake and they gathered together by the door. Ishi peered out to see what was happening. What he saw made his blood run cold. Large, military-style robots were breaking down doors and searching the area. Their metal heads grazed the top of the ceiling and their eyes glowed bright red as they scanned each person they came across. They didn't harm any of the citizen-servants, however, they were destroying pretty much everything else in there. An old man blocked their way, his hands gesturing wildly. Ishi winced, expecting the robots to kill the man, but they merely shoved him aside and kept moving through the rooms.

Ishi felt a hand on his shoulder and whipped around, thinking the robots had found them. Instead, he was greeted by Von who was frantically waving for them to follow him. He guided them to a set of stairs, which led down a series of tunnels. Before they knew it, they were under the city. In another city of its own. People were living down there and moving around as if they were on the street above. Bartering, chatting, some with their hands, others with their voices.

Von trudged through, insisting they keep up. Oslo had joined them and was bringing up the rear to make sure the children were protected on both sides. They came to a door and Von knocked three times, waited, then knocked four more. The door swung in and they were ushered into a cool dark space. A candle was lit and Ishi could see they were in a home of sorts. A tall, thin, black and gray-haired woman motioned for them to sit around a table. There was meat and cheese, along with warm tea. Von and the woman exchanged conversation with their hands for some time as the children sat and waited.

Oslo leaned forward. "This is Von's aunt. She will keep us safe while we are here."

The woman glanced over and smiled. "Welcome to my humble home."

"She can talk?" Ishi whispered.

"I can talk. My name is Nora. As Oslo said, I am Von's aunt. It is no longer safe for you to stay with him."

"Are you not a citizen-servant?" Ishi asked, then considered he might be being rude.

Nora shook her head. "I'm not. I refused years ago and was captured. I broke free and escaped back to the tunnels."

"Why didn't they come after you?" Jai asked, confused.

"For the most part, they stay out of the tunnels. These were old train tunnels. The concrete and metal walls mess up the robots' signals. The people won't come down here," Nora explained.

"Oh. Why don't the others come down here to live? The poor ones?" Ishi inquired.

Nora shrugged. "Some think they can change things up there, some are citizen-servants, and some can't breathe well down here. Not enough fresh air. The pollution settles in the tunnels. Many down here die from lung diseases."

"Why do you stay?" Ishi asked.

"Because it's better to be free down here than indentured up there."

Nora broke the meat and cheese up, handing each child a piece. She kissed Von on the cheek and handed him some, as well. Von went and sat next to Mara as they ate. She tried to converse with him, but he shook his head. He motioned to the cheese and made a sign for it with his hands. Mara repeated the sign and grinned. Von showed her a few more signs, then dug into his food.

After they ate, Nora asked the children to come to a sitting area. They found places to rest and waited. She and Von communicated, drawing Oslo in. When they stopped, they came over to the children.

"It isn't safe for you to stay with Von at the laundry anymore. At least not Oslo, Ishi, and Jai," Nora said. "I understand your trackers were removed but you must've been seen. Or we have a spy in our midsts. Either way, they know to look for you there. Von is no longer safe there, either, in the chance they know he was who transported you. He will stay with you. In the morning, you'll use the tunnel systems to get to where you need to go. There are still old maps posted at each station. No more trains, but you can walk along the tracks. I understand you're separating into two groups, yes?"

Ishi nodded. "Oslo and I are going to the Council. Jai and Mara are going to find Jai's mother."

Nora gazed at Jai. "I know of your mother. I'm sorry she didn't see what a gift she had in you."

Jai didn't reply but her eyes shined with tears. Nora came over and wrapped her arms around the thin girl. "They took my children. I had a son and a daughter. We ran when they were going to cut out our tongues. My husband protected us up until that point, but then he was killed. So we ran. However, my daughter had a hard time breathing down here, so we'd sneak up to get fresh air. On one of those excursions, we were spied and caught. We escaped and ran. I didn't see an open grate in the sidewalk and fell into the tunnels. They caught my children and I never saw them again. I'd like to believe they are still alive, but my heart tells me otherwise."

Jai clung to Nora as the woman told her tale. Nora didn't mind and rocked Jai back and forth like only a mother could. Von rose and motioned to Mara and Oslo to follow him to the other room. They were gone for some time and when they came back, Von's face was grim. Mara sat back down with the other children.

"Von is worried about our safety. He'll accompany me and Jai through the tunnels, so we do not get lost. This will leave just you and Oslo to go to the Council. Nora said she could go as far as the end of the tunnel but doesn't want to go up. Even so, Von said the likelihood of being captured is high and they'd want to make an example out of all of us."

"Does Von have a wife or children?" Ishi asked.

"No. Too risky. He doesn't want them getting trapped in the citizen-servant system. He'd like to remain with us if that's possible," Mara answered.

"Oh. I guess, but we don't even know where we are going or what will happen when we get there."

"He understands. I'm glad he is going with Jai and me. I was scared going alone."

Ishi watched Von standing in the corner, wondering what his life had been like before they met him. Von smiled, then turned to Nora. Their hands moved rapidly, Von pointing at the children. Nora frowned and sighed.

"Von told me he is going with you. I have some concerns, but he is headstrong and won't take no for an answer. So, I guess I'll be joining you through the tunnels, as well. Would that be alright?" Nora inquired.

"The more, the merrier," Mara replied.

"I'll go with Oslo and Ishi, Von will go with you girls. It will be safer that way. We'll head out in the morning. Get some rest. Oh, and do not leave my quarters tonight," Nora ordered.

"Why not?" Jai asked, her voice indignant.

"Not everyone in the tunnels has the best of intentions. Remember, you represent money to them. They could sell you or turn you in for money. Even if they seem nice, they're desperate. Desperate enough to hurt you. Don't forget that," Nora answered.

The following morning, they rose and packed what they could. Nora divided up the rest of her food between the two groups and drew a map for Von. He tucked it in his pack and the large group gathered together.

"We'll walk together until the tunnel splits. Then, Von will take Jai and Mara up to the performance center. Jai's mother is to sing there tonight. They'll wait for her to arrive, then confront her for what she did to Jai," Nora said.

"Then kill her," Jai whispered. Despite all their prodding, Jai wasn't budging on that.

Nora went on. "The other tunnel will get us close to the Council, however, not all the way. It's a block from the tunnel exit to the Council doors. It's extremely dangerous to be visible on the street but there is no way around it. Does everyone understand?"

The group nodded. They began the journey through the tunnels. More than once, a tunnel resident approached them, offering Nora money for the children. She carried a large dagger and waved it at them, telling them to back off. She was a force to be reckoned with. Ishi was secretly glad it was Nora going with Oslo and him, as she was fearless.

When they came to the tunnel split, the group sat and ate their last meal together for a while. Ishi glanced around at all their faces and wondered if they'd meet again. If all of them would survive.

If *any* of them would survive.

"It's time," Nora said, cutting the silence. "Finish up, we must get going. We can't stay in one place too long. Everyone has intentions and we can't wait to find out what those might be."

Oslo, Nora, and Ishi formed one group, while Von, Mara, and Jai formed another. They each stood at the mouth of their designated tunnel, staring at one another. Finally, Jai put her chin up and marched down the tunnel, forcing Mara and

Von to catch up to her. No goodbyes, no tears. Jai was on a mission. There was no going back.

Ishi watched them until he could no longer make out their shapes moving down the tunnel. He prayed they'd make it back safely. That they'd all make it back safely. This was only one part of the journey. Even if he made it to the Council, he still needed to convince someone, anyone, that the children on the island deserved help. If he couldn't, he needed to figure out another plan to save them. He turned and faced Nora and Oslo. Oslo used his eyes to shine a light down the dark tunnel, barely lighting their way.

Nora sighed and started down the path they needed to take to the Council. Ishi followed and Oslo walked behind to ensure no one attacked from that direction. With the three of them left, Ishi couldn't deny he felt a deep loss. As if part of his body had been removed. He'd felt the same when Timmy and Darius left. He didn't remember losing his birth family but having to leave this family broke his heart. He shoved the feeling down and pushed on. Now wasn't the time to think about what he'd lost, what he could lose. Now was the time to focus on what he needed to do to change the course of things.

He was doing this for all of them.

# Chapter Twenty-Seven

As they moved through the tunnel, Ishi wondered what they'd do once they got to the Council building. Clearly, he wouldn't be welcome there. They were marked and the robots were after them. At the bidding of humans. There was no one to trust. Ishi caught up with Nora and strode alongside her, thinking of the questions he needed to ask before they got there.

"Nora? Can I ask you something?"

Nora smiled down at him. "Of course. I can't promise I'll have any answers but ask away."

"Are there people in the Council who will help us or am I wasting my time?" Ishi asked.

"It's hard to say. There are people everywhere who work undercover to assist those of us The Service deems as unsatisfactory. They don't wear a special hat or anything, but they are there," Nora answered.

"How will I know who they are?"

"You won't. At least initially. They keep it under wraps well, due to circumstances. They can't blow their cover or they and their families will be murdered. Most likely, if you get assistance, you won't know where it came from."

"Oh."

"Don't give up hope. Oh, and one more thing. If someone seems to be outwardly helpful, don't trust them. Just as we have plants inside, so do they. They have people trained to pretend to be on our side, but are really gathering info to trap us," Nora warned.

Ishi's step faltered. He couldn't do this. He'd end up captured, or killed. He fell back and walked with Oslo, who'd been strangely quiet. Ishi didn't want to bother the robot. They matched steps down the tunnel when Oslo placed his hand on Ishi's shoulder, pausing his stride.

"I know you are scared, Ishmael, but you are strong and brave. You can do this," Oslo urged.

"How do you know? What if I get there and no one will listen?"

"They may not. You need to be prepared for that. However, you may find someone who will. There are also other options," Oslo said.

"What? What are they?" Ishi asked, feeling a small tinge of hope.

"The robots are programmed by humans but can be reprogrammed. If we can get into the system, we might be able to turn them to our side."

Ishi shook his head. "That sounds harder than trying to convince someone to listen. I don't know anything about computers. At all."

Oslo considered this, then began moving again. Ishi caught up with him. Oslo was quiet but Ishi could tell he was thinking hard. They turned down another tunnel, which ended at a ladder. Ishi frowned at Oslo for answers.

"This ladder goes up to the street. From there we have a block to go to get to the Council," Oslo explained.

"What happens when we get there?"

"I asked Von to reach out to his cousin, Bea. She works as a cleaner at the Council. She's expecting us. We'll need to go around to the delivery entrance," Nora chimed in, beginning the ascent up the ladder.

Ishi stared at her. "I thought you were only going this far, Nora?"

Nora grinned and shook her head. "I changed my mind. I want to be a part of this."

Ishi followed her and Oslo did his best to climb the thin metal rungs. He slipped a few times, but finally made it to the top.

At the street level, Nora pushed open a grate and peered out. Once she determined it was safe, she shoved it aside and climbed out, reaching back to give Ishi a hand. They both helped Oslo, though he was too heavy for them to do more than brace him.

The three stood on the street and Ishi felt very exposed. Nora gestured to an alley and they ducked into it, out of sight. From that vantage point, they were able to observe the people on the street.

Like before from the truck window, Ishi watched families with companion robots going about their day. Everyone seemed so detached, not making eye contact or speaking to one another. Not like the people in the tunnels, who laughed and talked almost nonstop.

Nora waited until the street was nearly empty, then motioned for them to follow her. Ishi wasn't sure. On the street it would be obvious they didn't fit in.

Nora paused and frowned at him. "Now or never. You've come this far, it's only a block. We can do this."

Ishi took a tentative step out of the alley, fully expecting to be struck by lightning. Nothing happened. Nora moved a little further and Oslo gently guided Ishi forward. Ishi knew the only way back was in front of him. Taking a deep breath, he strode up to Nora and nodded. She smiled and touched his cheek.

They drew some odd stares from people passing, but many assumed they were citizen-servants and ignored them. A security robot raised his hand for them to stop. Ishi was ready to bolt when Nora handed the robot a plastic card. The robot glanced at it, then waved them on. Ishi knew better than to ask, as Nora had made it clear they could not speak at all on the street.

The Council building loomed in front of them and Ishi's heart began to race. They scurried behind the building to the delivery entrance. As promised, within a few minutes Bea came to the door. She guided them in, scanning the alley behind them. Nora embraced her once they were inside and slipped Bea a packet. Bea smiled and sniffed the packet. Ishi tipped his head in confusion when Nora spoke.

"Herbs. We use them for healing. The card I handed the security robot showed I'm a citizen-servant. I'm not, but it isn't hard to come by with the right connections."

Bea tucked the packet into her apron and gestured for them to follow her. They moved through halls behind the walls and came out in a cafeteria. The food smelled divine and Ishi's stomach grumbled loudly. Bea smiled and slipped him a piece of bread and a potato. He gobbled it down in a couple of bites.

"Thank you."

Bea nodded. Then she went through the kitchen as they followed. They came to a cramped room with a table and chairs. Nora and Bea began communicating with their hands as Oslo translated.

"Bea said they have cracked down on insurgents. The people she knew here who were on our side have disappeared. She said there is one man who may still help. He is a Senator for the Southern territories Which includes the island you are from. She isn't sure he will still listen as it is a risk for him and his family, but it's worth a shot."

"Okay. Let's try," Ishi replied, finding his courage deep inside himself.

"Once the lunch service is done, Bea will take us up there through the hidden halls."

Ishi wanted to go now before he lost his bravery but trusted Bea knew what she was doing. He sat at the table and rested his head on the cool, wooden surface. He hadn't realized he dozed off until Nora shook him awake.

"It's time."

They moved silently through the hidden halls behind the walls until they came to a false wall. Bea pushed it open and went through, shutting it behind her. Ishi looked to Nora for information. She leaned in and whispered.

"She's making contact."

A few minutes later, Bea came back and communicated with Nora. Nora seemed unsure about the conversation but bobbed her head. "He's willing to see us. Something is off but we need to try."

"Is it alright?" Ishi asked.

"I sure hope so," Nora replied. "Stay close to Oslo."

They were escorted into a lavish room. A man in his forties was behind a grand, polished, wood desk. He waved his hand to a couple of chairs on the other side the desk, smiling. "Welcome, please have a seat."

Ishi sat, as did Nora. Oslo stood behind them. Bea disappeared back through the wall. The man rubbed his chin and sized them up. "My name is Burton Godfrey. As I understand it, you are here to file a complaint."

A complaint? Ishi worried the gravity of the situation hadn't been conveyed properly. "I'm trying to save the children on our island."

"Which island are you referring to?" Burton asked.

"Uh..." Ishi realized he didn't have a name to call it.

Thankfully, Oslo stepped in. "It is island A437B89."

The man typed on a computer and sighed. "Ah, yes, I see it here. Children's school run by Ms. Virginia. What seems to be the issue, son?"

"She's killing children. If they can't work or are ill. Or even if they challenge her, they disappear."

"I see. You are one of the children?"

Ishi nodded. "I was. I was supposed to get sent to an adult camp... well... that's what she told me, but now I know otherwise."

"Is that right? Why's that?"

"I turned sixteen."

The man's face flushed and he refused to make eye contact. "I see. Why didn't you go to the adult camp, then?"

Ishi glanced at Oslo. Did the man seriously not know? "Because there isn't an adult camp. They kill kids or work them to death once they turn sixteen."

Burton stared at his computer screen again, swallowing hard. "I don't know about all that. I'll look into it."

"Can you help us?" Ishi asked point blank. "Can you stop Ms. Virginia and the robots?"

Burton's eyes flicked toward Ishi, then away. "Sure, sure. I'll open an investigation. I thank you for bringing this to my attention. I have a nice lounge you can rest in and I'll have Bea bring you some refreshments. Let me see what I can do and I'll follow up with you shortly. Feel free to relax while I get this initiated."

Bea came back in and guided them to a room down the hall outside his door. Not the hidden halls, but the main halls. Burton was going to help them and they didn't need to hide anymore.

Bea paused at the door, putting her hand out to hold Nora back. Nora frowned and paused. Bea's hands moved nonstop. Then she looked at them, her face worried, and hurried down the hall.

Nora slipped a piece of fabric she tore off her skirt into the door jam, preventing it from locking. She tested it to make sure it could be opened. She turned to Oslo and Ishi, her face twisted in concern.

"Bea doesn't trust him. She was told to lock us in here, but she told me to make sure the door didn't clip. She didn't say why, she just has a sense that he wasn't being honest. She was listening on the other side of the wall."

"Are we in trouble?" Ishi asked.

Nora didn't have time to answer before it became abundantly clear they were indeed in trouble.

Alarms went off all over the building.

# Chapter Twenty-Eight

"W hat do we do now?" Ishi asked, the thunder of robot feet coming down the hall.

Nora peered out of the door and waved for Ishi and Oslo to come close. "We need to go. Bea said there is access to the secret tunnels down the hallway in a supply closet if we can make it there. Follow me!"

Nora was through the door before her last word hit the air and Oslo pushed Ishi from behind. They needed to move. Once in the hallway, Ishi could see robots descending on them and the man, Burton, was watching from his doorway. He didn't look happy, he even seemed apologetic.

They ran in the other direction, Ishi tripping over his cane. Oslo caught him and practically carried him to the supply closet. They bolted in and locked the door behind them. It wouldn't stop the robots, but it might slow them down. Nora began feeling along the walls, searching for the hidden door, but came up empty-handed.

"Damnit, I can't find it. Oslo, are you able to scan to see if you can pick up anything hollow?" Nora asked.

Oslo stepped into the middle of the room, adjusting his eyes to scan. He worked his way around the room, then stopped. "It is not here."

"It has to be! Bea said there was a way from the supply closet to the hidden pathways," Nora exclaimed.

"Could it be in the ceiling or the floor?" Ishi asked.

Nora's eyes lit up. "Good thinking! Oslo can you scan those, too?"

Loud banging came at the door and it became apparent it would only be minutes before the robots broke through. Oslo was scanning the floor, then shifted his gaze to the ceiling. He stopped, the beams landing on one of the tiles.

"There. That is a false ceiling."

Nora scrambled to find something to climb on, discovering a step ladder. "It's not tall enough to get us all the way through, but I can get up and push the tile away."

The door behind them began to splinter and Ishi felt his heart racing in his chest. "Hurry!"

Nora climbed up and shoved the tile away. She pulled herself up through the opening and stretched back down for Ishi. "Give me your hand!"

Ishi got on the step ladder and reached up for Nora's hands. She grasped him and began to pull with all her might. Oslo lifted from underneath until Ishi was safely in the ceiling. The robot climbed on the ladder, as Ishi and Nora reached for him. They struggled to budge him, but as the door busted down into the supply room, the three of them found a strength they didn't know they had. Oslo leapt up, giving them the ability to drag him through the opening the rest of the way. The robots below tried to follow but the step ladder collapsed under their weight. This gave the trio a chance to reposition the ceiling tile and crawl away from the opening.

They moved through the tunnel until they came to another room. Nora peered down. "It's the citizen-servants' quarters."

"They live here?" Ishi asked, confused.

"Not exactly. They often have to work long shifts and don't have time to go home, so they have beds and a kitchen here. Let's go in."

"Is it safe?"

"Not really, but we can't keep climbing through the ceiling space. We don't want Oslo falling through."

As if Oslo was testing that theory, the rafter they were on began to creak ominously. He bobbed his head and shifted off the beam. "Good idea."

They slipped through the tile into the room and peered around. It was empty. Nora checked the door and locked it. Everyone must have gone out because of the alarm. She plopped down on one of the beds and stared at Oslo.

"We can't stay here long. They'll be checking all the rooms. We need to find a way out of the building," she said.

"We can't! I haven't found help yet," Ishi insisted.

"Ishi, I know you want to find someone who will listen, but at this point, we're in danger. They'll kill you and me, then turn Oslo into scrap. Maybe we need to go back down into the tunnels to regroup," Nora countered.

"No! We're running out of time. Now everyone knows I'm trying to stop Ms. Virginia. If I don't do something soon, she might kill all the children just to spite me and cover her tracks. Please! There has to be another way!"

Nora threw her hands up in the air. "Oslo?"

Oslo was quiet, his head low. "No one here is going to assist us. Especially now that our presence has been announced to everyone. No one else will be willing to take the risk, as it puts their and their families' lives on the line. We are on our own from here. Even you, Nora, should go back home."

"No, I'm here for you. I have nothing left down there. I've been hiding my whole life. It's time to stay and fight. What's plan B?"

"Plan B?" Ishi asked.

"You know, if the first plan doesn't work, what's your next move?"

Ishi panicked, he didn't have a plan B. "I don't know. This is all new to me."

"We need to hack into the computer system. This location controls many of the robots in the region. All of them here at the Council. If we can get into the system, we may be able to shut down the robots. The humans are nothing without them," Oslo offered.

"I don't know anything about computers," Ishi complained.

"Me either," Nora added.

"We will cross that bridge when we get there. First, we must find the hub."

They stared at each other, no one knowing how they were going to do that when a soft knock came at the door. Nora frowned and went to the door, listening intently. It was silent. The knock came again and Nora shrugged, opening the door a crack. It was Bea. Nora let her in and shut the door behind her. They embraced and Bea began talking with her hands. Nora replied and Oslo joined in. Ishi watched in amazement as their hands flew a million miles a minute. Finally, Nora turned to Ishi.

"She is going to lead us to the computer room. We need to go now, while the hallway is empty."

They gathered by the door, aware they needed to move as soon as it opened. Nora swung the door open and Bea rushed out with the rest of them on her heels. They ran down the hall and turned a corner, to see a group of robots searching rooms. The machines spied the interlopers and rushed toward them. Nora moved out in front, waving her arms.

"Here we are! Come and get us!"

The robots stormed toward Nora, and she turned to the rest of them. "Run!"

Bea took off in the other direction and Ishi and Oslo paused, not wanting to leave Nora behind. She met their eyes in desperation. "Go now!"

They faltered, then realized there was no option. They bolted down the hallway, hitting the next corridor. Ishi spun back to see the robots surround Nora and drive her to the ground. She wasn't moving. He wanted to go back to save her, but Oslo shoved him forward.

"Ishmael, it is too late. We need to go."

"But Nora..."

"She knew what she was doing, she wants you to change things. So change things!" Oslo ordered.

Heartbroken and demoralized, Ishi hustled after Bea, picturing Nora's lifeless body on the ground. He never wanted anyone to get hurt. He ignored the hot tears on his face and stayed within arm's length of Bea as she weaved down various hallways. Finally, she came to a door and opened it, gesturing for them to go inside. They darted in and were surrounded by massive computers. Bea locked the door behind them. It was all foreign to Ishi, so he looked at Oslo for guidance.

Oslo walked around the room, looking at monitors. He rotated back to Ishi. "We need to get in and change the programming."

"Can't we just smash them?" Ishi asked.

"No, the robots already have been programmed, smashing the computers will not change that. They will continue on course. We need to change their messages."

Ishi wanted to cry. They'd made it so far, yet he nor Oslo knew how to reprogram their robots. If only Timmy were here, he knew everything about computers. "Oslo, we need Timmy."

Oslo tipped his head. "Let me see if I can contact his doctors."

Oslo went to one of the computers and pulled out a cord of some kind from his neck. He plugged it into the computer and went into a trance. Bea and Ishi stood helplessly as Oslo began humming and rocking back and forth. Ishi had no idea what was happening. The computer Oslo was attached to lit up and lights began flashing around them. All of sudden, a series of sounds erupted from the computer and Oslo returned them. This went on for a couple of minutes between Oslo and the computer.

As quickly as it started, it stopped and Oslo came back to life. He spun toward Ishi, his eyes a shade of blue Ishi had never seen. Oslo seemed to still be detached from himself and a strange static was coming from his mouth. It wasn't Oslo speaking, rather it seemed like he was acting like a conduit. But for what? Ishi moved closer, listening to the static. Behind the static, another sound emerged. Faint. It sounded like a voice.

"Hello?" Ishi asked into Oslo's mouth.

The voice was coming through sporadically but Ishi swore he heard his name. He leaned in even closer, almost touching Oslo's mouth. "Hello?"

The voice was stronger but still broken. "Is-i, that you? Hear me?"

Ishi almost fainted with the realization and grasped Oslo's shoulders as he recognized the voice.

Timmy!

# Chapter Twenty-Nine

"Timmy! I can't believe it!" Ishi exclaimed. Last he'd heard, Timmy was in a coma. Oslo was not able to tell him how he was able to get Timmy on the line, as he was acting as a bridge between them. Ishi had so many questions but knew Timmy was weak and the line could cut at any time. "I miss you!"

"I... miss... you, too," Timmy whispered, his voice slow and faint. "You need... computer help?"

"We do. We're trapped in this computer room. We need to disable the robots to stop them from attacking. Can you guide me?"

The line fell silent and Ishi was afraid either the connection had dropped or Timmy couldn't help. He heard a shallow breath, followed by a cough. Then another familiar voice came on the line.

"Ishi, it's Dari. Timmy can't talk much more. He's going to write directions down in my Braille translator, and I'll tell you what he wrote. Can you ask yes or no or simple questions?"

Ishi frowned. He didn't know how he could ask yes or no questions because he wasn't even sure where to begin. He scanned the room, then described what he was seeing over the line. "There are four large computers and several monitors attached to them. They are on, but I don't know what I'm looking for."

He heard tapping and realized Timmy was inputting instructions for Dari to translate from his Braille machine. Afraid they'd lose the line before he got the information, Ishi drummed his fingers impatiently.

Dari came back on. "Timmy asked if on any of the monitors there is an icon called control panel?"

Ishi peered at each screen and saw an icon on the second one that said control center. "Not control panel, but control center."

"Open that and tell us what you see."

Ishi clicked on it and a list came up. Each said something to the effect of crob1 to crob101 and on endlessly. "I see a list of maybe robots?"

Muttering and tapping went on again. Dari cleared his throat. "Can you select them all?"

Ishi stared at the screen, confused. "Uh, at the top there is a dropdown for actions?"

A loud banging came at the door and Ishi knew they were running out of time. He clicked on the actions tab and it opened options of disable, redirect, available, recenter, reprogram. "I see lots of options but they are breaking down the door! What do I do? Disable them?"

"Yes, Timmy says disable all of them. Can you select all?" Dari asked.

Ishi clicked around seeing he could select groups but not all. "No, only groups. I don't have time!"

"Do any of them say Council or Headquarters?"

Ishi saw HQ by some of the groups. "HQ?"

"Timmy says yes! Disable those quickly!" Dari ordered.

The door began to bend inward and Ishi clicked all the groups that said HQ next to them. He then clicked the disable and submit buttons. As soon as he did, the banging outside the door fell silent. Bea opened the door and peered out. Ishi rotated and could see robots on the ground in the hallway.

"Now what?" he murmured over the line.

More tapping. "Timmy says it's temporary. They may be able to reactivate them from another location. They still need to be reprogrammed, but only he can do that or someone with that knowledge and time. You need to get out of there and get to safety before they undo the change. Timmy is going to see if he can reprogram them from here. He needs to rest but as soon as he can, he'll get to a computer system and try."

Ishi didn't want to disconnect but knew Timmy was exhausted and needed to conserve his strength. "I love you and Timmy, Dari. Please, tell him that. I miss you both so much. How long do we have?"

"He doesn't know. He said to destroy those computers, so they can't just come in and reactivate them. Are you able to do that?"

"I can. Thank you. I'll see you soon."

The line went dead and Ishi fought back grief. Oslo came to and nodded. "We must do this."

They began smashing the computers as Bea stood guard at the door. As soon as they were sure all the computers were inoperable, she led them back through the hidden halls to an outside exit. Ishi turned to her.

"Do you want to come with us?"

Bea smiled, tipping her head. She gestured to Oslo and he gestured back. He turned to Ishi. "She will come. Her parents are gone and she has been staying with friends, however, she is ready to go."

Ishi liked Bea and grinned. "I'm glad to hear that. How old are you, Bea?"

She signed to Oslo, who answered Ishi. "Seventeen."

"I'm sixteen," Ishi replied, realizing he was indeed sixteen. In all the travels, he'd forgotten to acknowledge his birthday. Being alive was enough to celebrate, at least for now.

The three scurried down the road into the tunnels. They went back to Nora's quarters and slipped inside. Ishi collapsed on her thin cot. Oslo sat in a chair made from crates and Bea began rifling through the makeshift cabinets. She took out some dried bread and a can of ancient beans. Without being asked, she heated the meager meal and handed Ishi a plate. They ate in silence, reflecting on the events of the day.

Oslo zoned out and Ishi knew he was receiving another message. He waited as Oslo was in the state and once Oslo came back to their reality, Ishi watched intently.

"Well?"

"Well, what?" Oslo asked.

"Did you get a message?"

"Yes. It is not good, Ishmael," Oslo said.

"What do you mean?"

"The man you talked to. Burton? He tipped off the authorities and they are sending robots to the island. To eliminate the problem."

"The problem? Ms. Virginia?"

Oslo shook his head. "No, they do not see Ms. Virginia as the problem."

"Then who? I'm not there, so it can't be me," Ishi replied, wracking his brain to understand.

Oslo did his robot sigh. "Ishi, the way they see it, is you would not have come and caused them trouble if it was not for the other children on the island."

"Wait... are you saying they are going after the other children?" Ishi asked, horrified.

"It appears so. We need to leave if we are to get there in time," Oslo said.

"What about Jai and Mara?"

"We may not have time. We need to go now."

Ishi pushed down the panic rising in his chest and shook his head. "I messed this all up, didn't I?"

"No, Ishi. You did what you needed to do and you are up against an army. Without reprogramming the robots, they will destroy the island, the children, whatever else they decide is a threat."

Ishi pounded his fist against the mattress, which was only a couple of stacked blankets. "What do I do, now? How do I fix this?"

Oslo watched him, his face expressionless. "I do not know. Maybe Timmy can get them reprogrammed."

It was a long shot. A really long shot. He leaned over and vomited beside the cot, the little bit of food he'd just eaten coming back up almost like it went down. He glanced at Bea, who was listening, concerned. He forgot because she couldn't talk, that she could still hear.

Oslo zoned out again. Ishi got up and shook him, but the robot remained inert. "Oslo! Oslo!"

Oslo didn't reply. He was receiving another message. Ishi plopped down on the mattress and stared at Bea. "I'm sorry I got you into this. Maybe it would be better if you went back to your home."

Bea shook her head. She made a motion with her hands. Ishi frowned, trying to understand. She did it again. One motion looked like no. The other he was unsure about. She did it again and waved around the space. Ishi understood. She had no real home, no real family.

He nodded and glanced back at Oslo. Whatever he was receiving, it wasn't good. He could see Oslo's eyes shifting back and forth like he was stressed. Ishi wished he could see inside Oslo's mind. Comprehend what he was seeing. He focused back on Bea.

"Can you teach me how you communicate? So I can understand what you are saying?"

Bea moved beside him and every time he'd say something, she'd repeat it with her hands. He'd say a word and she'd make the sign. They did this for some time until Oslo came out of his trance. Oslo jumped up and peered around. He went to the door and gazed out, his eyes shining bright purple. Seeing it was clear, he went out and walked down the tunnel. After a moment, he came back.

"Oslo, what's going on?" Ishi asked, confused by the robot's strange behavior.

Oslo didn't answer. He tilted his head like he was listening out for something. Then, as if he heard what he was listening for, he whipped around and faced Bea and Ishi.

"We must go. Bea, is there another way out of the tunnels?"

Bea chewed her lip and motioned out the door. Oslo looked and shook his head. Bea got up and walked to the door, pointing to the tracks. She made a quick gesture Oslo understood.

He turned to Ishi. "We will need to go down on the tracks into the electrical tunnel. It is the only way out."

"I don't understand. Why can't we go out the way we came in?" Ishi asked.

"It is not safe. They are not only after us anymore," Oslo replied, his voice thick with concern.

"Who are they after?"

"They are blaming the citizen-servants for us breaking into the Council and disabling the robots. They are going after them, as well."

"What does that mean? What are they going to do to them?" Ishi questioned, afraid he already knew the answer.

"They are going to eradicate them all."

# Chapter Thirty

They hustled down the tracks, hearing loud booms behind them. It sounded like the tunnels were being blown up. Ishi hoped it wasn't so, he never intended to get anyone else involved in his quest. He thought about Jai, Von, and Mara, manifesting they were somewhere safe.

The tunnel parallel to the train track narrowed where the wires went into a smaller tunnel. Bea motioned for them to follow and they hunched down to fit. Oslo got stuck a few times but they were able to wiggle him loose. Just when Ishi was afraid they wouldn't be able to go any further, the tunnel opened into a large room with machines. The electrical wires ran into them and Ishi realized it was computers to run the trains. Or had been. The trains didn't run anymore and hadn't for some time.

"Are we safe?" Ishi inquired, his voice shaking.

"For now. They cannot get in the way we did, but they can come in through the outside entrance," Oslo answered.

Ishi peered around, spying a metal door on the far side. "Is that the door? Can we get out through it?"

Bea nodded, then made a gesture with her hands. Oslo made a motion back to her and tipped his head. "We can, but we need to wait until it calms down out there. That door goes to a ladder, which goes right up the street."

"How long do we have to wait?"

"I do not know. I need to tap into these computers and see if I can intercept any communication. Rest while I do that and we will talk after," Oslo instructed. He went to the computers and plugged himself into the main one. Like before, he seemed to go vacant and Ishi knew the conversation was over. For now.

Bea sat and leaned against the wall. Ishi stared at Oslo, wondering if someone would show up and find them. The computers were still active, so they must monitor them somehow. For what reason, he wasn't sure. He closed his eyes and thought about Timmy and Darius. What they were doing. Oslo making a strange sound snapped him out of his imagery and he opened his eyes. Oslo was distressed.

"Oslo? Is everything alright?"

Oslo yanked his cord free from the computer and shook his head. "No, we need to go now. They are after Jai."

"After Jai? Why? How?" Ishi asked. He knew the authorities we searching for them, but this was super specific.

Oslo stared at him, wordless. Ishi understood. Jai had done what she came to do. He couldn't believe it. He leapt up and grabbed his bag. "Where is she?"

"They are searching for her around the concert hall. Bea, can you get us there?" Oslo asked.

Bea frowned and stood up. She bobbed her head but was also communicating with her hands. Oslo tapped his metal chin with his fingered hand, then nodded. "You are right. The more of us there, the more likely we are to get caught. We may not have a choice, though. Can you get us close?"

Bea nodded and went to the door. It was risky, however, Jai was in danger. They opened the door and climbed the ladder up to the street. Night was beginning to fall, which would give them some cover. However, there were also mandatory curfews in place, so anyone out after dark was sure to draw attention.

They sidled along the wall of the building where they came out and ducked into doorways to hide whenever they saw someone else. They did this for a few blocks when sirens went off everywhere. Startled, Bea ran into an alley for cover. Oslo and Ishi followed, the three hunching down by a dumpster. The sirens ended abruptly, making the night still and almost too quiet. They crept back out to the street and peered around.

The street was empty. No cars, no robots, no people. Ishi sighed, considering what that meant. Was it a good or a bad thing? Bea seemed unsure, as well.

"How far are we from the concert hall?" Ishi asked.

Bea pointed down the street and held up two fingers.

"Two blocks?"

She bobbed her head. They began a slow crawl toward the concert hall, jumping at every sound. They came around the corner on the second block and paused, seeing lights ahead. The concert hall was completely surrounded and an army of large, military robots was ready and waiting around the perimeter. If Jai was in there, she wasn't getting out.

"What do we do, Oslo?" Ishi whispered.

"Nothing," the robot replied.

"Nothing? But Jai, Mara, and Von are in there!" Ishi countered.

"And we are out here. We must wait."

Ishi didn't want to stop, but he could see Oslo's point. The building was surrounded and the tunnels had been destroyed. So they waited.

After about an hour, some of the military disbanded, leaving less than half to stand guard. Oslo, Bea, and Ishi found a grove of trees to hide in, at a park close to the building. Ishi knew they couldn't hold off going back to the island forever, but he couldn't bear to leave Jai, either. She'd made her decision but she deserved to have a life. Frustrated, he scanned around. Bea was sleeping, Oslo was resting against a tree.

Ishi stood up, creeping toward the opening of trees, and watched. The remaining robot soldiers stood silently, ready to pounce. The rest of the authorities had dispersed or gone inside the building.

It was now or never.

Ishi grabbed his cane and headed to the line of robots. He pretended he couldn't speak and made gestures at them with his hands. One of them raised a weapon at Ishi's head and that's when the panic set in.

A voice to the right called out. "Halt. Leave the boy alone."

Ishi turned to the voice and was surprised to see Burton Godfrey, the man from the Council. Burton rapidly approached Ishi, guiding him away by his shoulder. "Keep moving. I'll explain."

Ishi jerked his shoulder away, turning on the man. "You did this! You let them know we were there. You killed Nora!"

"I did and I *am* sorry. You need to understand, all of us are at risk. My family is at risk. One by one, people like me have been disappearing. Or worse, finding their families dead. I didn't want to set off the alarm, but I needed them to know I was someone they could trust, so they'd leave my family alone. It's not right, but I'd do it again," Burton explained.

"Why should I trust you now?"

"You shouldn't, but what choice do you have?"

Ishi deflated. He had no choice. Burton could have him killed on the spot. "I just want to get my friend out of there and go home."

"Is your friend the one that killed the singer Mimi Diamond?"

Mimi Diamond? Ishi assumed that was Jai's mother. "I think so. That was her mother who tried to kill her."

"Is that right? Well, Ms. Diamond has a spear through the brain now. Your friend? Where is she?" Burton asked.

"If I knew that, we wouldn't be here right now. I'm trying to find her."

Burton paused and stared back at the concert hall. "I have an idea. I know you don't trust me and that's fine. However, I have some pull around here. I need you to follow my lead."

Ishi scowled at the man, who only a few hours ago was willing to have them all murdered. "What's in it for you?"

"Believe it or not, I want to help you. My family comes first but they are safe, hidden, so I want to make things right."

Ishi didn't have much choice and glanced over to where Oslo and Bea were hiding. If they hadn't already noticed he slipped away, they would soon. Time was running out. "Fine."

Burton put his hand on Ishi's shoulder again, this time more firmly. He guided him to the line of robots and flashed a badge. "I got this one. I'm going to interrogate him into telling me where the others are."

The robots stared blankly but didn't try to stop him as Burton breached the line with Ishi, heading up the large concrete stairs. Ishi stumbled a few times but Burton's hand on his shoulder kept him upright. Burton's fingers were digging in painfully to Ishi's shoulder and he tried to wriggle away.

"Don't move," Burton whispered. "This has to look real."

Ishi still didn't trust Burton, but at least he was getting into the building. They maneuvered through the tall, glass doors around a group of soldiers and onto an elevator. Burton pressed the eighth-floor button and let go of Ishi's shoulders. "Let me do any talking."

The doors slid open, and they were in a massive room with no interior walls. Burton motioned for Ishi to wait and approached a group of suited men surrounded by military robots. He began speaking in low tones to them, glancing every now and then at Ishi. They all began looking at Ishi.

When they turned back to one another, Ishi took his chance and ran down a hall, hiding in a small utility closet. As soon as Burton and the other men realized Ishi was gone, an alarm went off. Ishi held his breath, hearing the thunder of feet coming down the hall. He felt along the closet walls, relieved to find a latch. He slid it open, revealing a false wall like in the Council. The citizen-servants had been creating escapes everywhere. Ishi slid into the opening and shut the door behind him.

He'd made it a distance when the tunnel abruptly dropped and he found himself falling down some sort of chute. The chute came to a sudden stop and he fell a few feet onto something both hard and soft.

"Ow!" a small voice cut through the blackness.

Ishi fumbled in his pack for the light Nora had given him and clicked it on. A pair of large, frightened, yet angry, eyes stared back at him.

"Turn it off, Ishi."

"Jai? Is that you?" Ishi asked, cutting the light.

"Who else would it be?"

# Chapter Thirty-One

Ishi hugged her so hard, she grunted in response. He eased up and sat back, trying to make out her face in the dark. "I'm so glad you're alright."

Jai shrugged. "Right as rain."

Ishi had never heard the saying and frowned. "Rain? How is rain right?"

"I don't know. My mother used to say that. Guess she'll never say it again."

Ishi swallowed hard. "Did you kill your mother, Jai?"

"I said I would."

That much was true. Jai never wavered from her goal of killing her mother. Ishi hoped once she came face to face with the woman who bore her, she'd find some compassion. Not that her mother deserved compassion, rather for Jai's own sake and mental sanity.

"I see. Do you want to talk about it?" Ishi asked.

"Do you want to hear about it?" Jai countered.

He didn't, but knew it needed to come out, eventually. "When you are ready to tell me. Where are Von and Mara?"

Jai sighed. "When I killed my mother... before really, Mara went to see if she could get in communication with you."

"Oh. I don't think Oslo got any communication," Ishi replied, thinking back to if Oslo had said anything. If Oslo heard from them, he didn't tell Ishi.

"He didn't, she couldn't. She and Von got trapped on the upper level, while I slipped behind the stage."

"Where are they now?"

"I don't know. I haven't seen them since. I crawled into the vent after, well, you know. I've been hiding until you fell on top of me." Jai coughed in the dark and Ishi tried to see where they were.

"Do you know how to get out of here?" Ishi asked, clicking on the light.

"No. I ended up here just like you. I was in the tunnels, then it spit me out here."

Ishi shined the light around them. Above them was the vent they came through. Around them was just a metal tomb. No other way in or out. "Damn."

Jai peered up and shrugged, oddly nonplussed, considering the situation they were in. "Seems about right. Any ideas?"

Ishi shook his head. "Not really. Why does the vent come out here?"

They felt around, seeing what the purpose of the space would be. The floor below them was a grate and Ishi shined the light toward it. He leaned forward and peered down through the tiny holes in the grate.

Below them was a larger room. A ceremonial room it appeared like. "Jai, help me lift this grate. I think we can drop down into that room."

They felt around the edges until they found a small lifted area of the metal they could get their fingers under. They pulled up a section of the grate and scanned the space. It was empty. Ishi lowered Jai into the room, then eased himself down as best he could, still hitting the floor harder than he intended.

Staring back up at the space, he frowned. "Well, that's weird. Why do you think there's that space up there?"

Jai scrunched her face and narrowed her eyes at the grate. "It looks like some kind of cage. But for what?"

Ishi sighed. "I don't understand this world. This room is weird, too, don't you think? Look at those odd symbols on the wall."

They moved to the wall and ran their hands over the symbols etched into the concrete. An idea dawned on Ishi. "Where did you find the tunnels that led here?"

"There was a door in the stage room."

"A door, or a vent?"

"A door. It was like a trapdoor but in the wall," Jai answered.

"What if that wasn't only a tunnel? It felt like I was going down a slide. It wasn't like any tunnel I've been in. It was like it was meant to be there, to end at the tomb room."

"Yeah, it was strange."

Ishi stared up and realized it was a trap of some kind. It was meant to capture people like him and Jai. The room they were in was directly under the vent and at their feet was a huge symbol. As if they were performing rituals in there.

"We need to get out of here. This is a bad place," Ishi whispered. He felt along the walls until he sensed a give. "Here, I think this panel is a door."

Jai came over and they pressed all over the panel, trying to find a way to open it. Nothing seemed to be working. There was no way out. Ishi pounded against the door, then immediately regretted it. Footsteps came from the other side and he could hear them congregating outside the panel.

"Ishi! They found us!" Jai exclaimed, sounding afraid for the first time in a long time.

"Shhh. Maybe they'll go away."

They didn't. He could hear the panel being opened and he and Jai ran to the other side of the room. There was a giant, ornate chair they hid behind. The door swung open and four large robots stepped into the room. Ishi held his breath, glancing at Jai. She was squatted down, grasping the legs of the chair in her hands. Small, delicate hands that killed her own mother.

The robots began to move through the room, turning over furniture and scouring the area for the source of the noise. As they approached the chair Ishi and Jai were hiding behind, Ishi closed his eyes, preparing for the inevitable.

"Looking for something?" a sarcastic voice from the doorway said.

The robots turned to the sound and Jai and Ishi peered out. Mara and Von! The robots rushed the door, but Mara didn't move. As they approached her, she held out some kind of metal stick. The first robot went to swipe the stick away, but its body began to jerk and spark. It fell and the next one came at Mara. This time, Von jumped out of the shadows and hit the robot with another stick. It collapsed like the first one. The other two were quickly disabled as well.

"Ishi!" Mara exclaimed, running to hug him. They embraced and Jai came out, as well. Mara watched her, her eyes unreadable, then smiled. "I'm glad you're alright."

"Where did you get those sticks?" Ishi asked.

Mara and Von glanced at each other, then Mara turned to Ishi. "They use these to discipline citizen-servants. We found them in one of the rooms."

"Discipline? That would kill someone!" Jai yelled.

Von nodded and made a motion with his hands. Mara translated. "That's their intent."

Ishi glanced up at the grate again and pointed. "Does this have anything to do with that?"

Von's eyes followed Ishi's hand and he shuddered. He signed to Mara and she gasped. "Von says they perform ceremonies and sacrifice whoever they put in there."

"That's horrible!" Ishi said.

"That's not the worst of it. This is the concert hall. They do it for entertainment. Not for the masses but the special VIPs," Mara translated.

"Who? Who do they do it to?" Ishi asked.

Mara looked at Von. He appeared ill and made one motion. Mara stared at Von, not wanting to share what he told her. She turned to Ishi and Jai. "The base class. The poor. Sometimes citizen-servants who they feel have gotten out of line. Many times... children."

"Children?" Jai asked, her voice trembling with horror.

Von nodded, wiping tears from his eyes. Mara went over and wrapped her arms around him. Citizen-servants were considered the second class, but it was clear that was only the case when they behaved and didn't challenge the upper class.

"We need to go," Ishi whispered, ready to leave that horrible room. "I need to find Oslo and Bea."

"Bea? What happened to Nora?" Mara asked.

"She... she died saving us. The robots killed her at the Council. Bea was Von's contact at the Council. So, Bea came with us when we escaped. She is also a citizen-servant. We got into a computer room and disabled the robots there to get out. The people, the elite, I guess, are going after citizen-servants for aiding us."

Von's face dropped and he made a frantic gesture at Mara, who nodded and faced the children. "Von and I need to go. He needs to find his family."

"Aren't you coming with us?" Ishi asked.

Mara smiled at Von, taking his hand. "No. I'm staying with Von. He's my family now."

Ishi could see the growing love between them and sighed. "I understand. Please warn them to arm themselves. They're no longer protected."

Von bobbed his head and touched his heart. He let go of Mara's hand and came over to embrace Ishi. He stepped back and gestured with his hands. Ishi stared at Mara for an explanation since she seemed to understand his communication.

"Von says you are brave and admires your strength to stand up to them. He wishes he had done that much sooner, but he is willing to do that now. You must go and save the children, he must go and save his people. Thank you, Ishi. We both are grateful for your strength."

"Mara, what about you?"

"My people are dead. I will fight alongside Von. Please go, before more of them come. I promise we'll find each other again. Now, you and Jai go!"

Ishi didn't want to leave them but knew Mara was right. It was only a matter of time before more robots or people came. He touched Jai's arm and she nodded. They ran out of the room down a darkened hallway, until they got to a flight of stairs. Above them, it sounded like all hell had broken loose. Ishi put his head down, grasped Jai's hand, and bolted up the stairs. His leg was throbbing but he was determined. They got to the top of the stairs and ran into a wall of robots. Just as the robots were ready to fire on them, something strange occurred.

The robots crumpled to the ground, their lights going out. Each one was nothing more than a hunk of metal on the floor, revealing a surprise.

Oslo and Bea stood behind them, holding a machine Ishi had never seen.

A portable control center.

# Chapter Thirty-Two

"We must go!" Oslo yelled, leading the way out of the space. He disabled robots as they went, rotating back to the children. "The range is not broad, but stick close to me and we can make it through."

The children formed a tight-knit group and trailed Oslo closely. Ishi glanced back, hoping to see Mara and Von, but they were gone. Likely ducked into the walls to get to his people. *Their* people. In a way, Ishi envied them. For finding each other, for finding a reason to fight together. He only hoped they'd win.

The group made it outside, robots falling around them like wheat being cut by a scythe. They made a direct line for the port, praying the portable computer would hold up. There were a slew of boats of different sizes and shapes in the marina, bobbing on the waves. Oslo scanned around and decided on one, rushing toward it.

"Oslo, we don't have keys," Ishi stated.

"We do not need them," Oslo countered. He went to the engine and extracted a thin flat blade from his chest. He inserted it in the keyhole and turned it. The engine sputtered but didn't start. Ishi glanced back at the land and the robots they'd disabled were coming to and rising from the ground.

"Uh, Oslo?"

Oslo tracked where Ishi was looking, then nodded. "Unfortunately, it only freezes them in range. Once we are out of range, they can come to."

"I miss Timmy," Ishi muttered. Not just for that, however, Timmy's ability to manipulate computer systems was unmatched.

"Me too," Oslo agreed. He turned the makeshift key again and the engine roared to life. "Untie the boat!"

Jai and Ishi scrambled to the ropes, eyeing the approaching robots. Bea joined them and the three of them managed to unwind the ropes as the robots hit the dock. They shoved off into the water, creating a gap between them and the robots. Oslo steered the boat out to the open ocean, not looking back. The robots stopped at the edge of the dock, watching them depart. Behind the robots came a swarm of citizen-servants, the bottom class, and those who secretly supported them in an unmatched rage. One by one, robots were disabled and dismantled.

Jai opened her mouth and let out a sound that resembled a war cry. Ishi stared at her, then joined in. As the land shrunk in the distance, he felt hope for the first time. Their presence *had* changed things. Not for the better initially, but it put the wheels in motion. Now, he needed to get back to the island. He needed to get Timmy and Darius home.

They fell to silence as they hit nothing but the expansive sea. Ishi considered how they'd handle things once they got back to the island. Oslo's computer could give them a safe path... he hoped. Ishi went to Oslo.

"Will the computer work on the island?" he asked.

Oslo tipped his head. "I am not sure. Maybe, but considering the island is far from the mainland, I do not know if it will. We need to have a backup plan if it doesn't, or it loses power."

Another backup plan? Ishi knitted his brow and thought. If the computer didn't work, the robots and Ms. Virginia would be waiting for them when they arrived. They tracked all boats that came to the island. Ishi gazed at the computer and had an idea. "Can the computer break the signal of us coming to the island?"

Oslo thought about it. "It could, but again, it depends on if it will work out there. We can try."

"If it doesn't, is there a way we can get onto the island without them knowing?"

"We can swim," Jai said from behind them. "Or use the liferaft."

Ishi wasn't keen on swimming but the liferaft might work. "Oslo can you try to break the signal, so we can get close? If not, then we can take the raft."

"Yes, but I cannot get on the raft. I am too heavy for that one. The other raft had a wood base and was larger," Oslo replied.

Ishi shuddered. He needed Oslo. Oslo couldn't get in the water and couldn't get on the raft. "What if you were spread out over the raft?"

"Like in pieces?" Oslo asked, a tinge of humor in his voice.

"Yes, disburse the weight," Ishi said.

"That might work. I cannot say for sure, but it is worth trying."

They worked out the plan, praying it wouldn't be necessary. As they neared the island within a few miles, far enough out to not attract attention, Oslo tried the computer.

Oslo shook his head. "The computer is not responding. Inflate the raft."

They hustled to the side of the boat where the raft was and pulled the cord, inflating it. They tied it off to the side of the boat and Ishi looked at Oslo. Oslo looked grim but nodded.

"You need to remember how to put me back together. Only remove the appendages and my head. Keep my torso intact. This is where my system is. I can keep operating as long as that is kept running."

"Okay," Ishi whispered, his voice giving away his fear. He approached Oslo and placed his hand on the robot's chest. "You are my family, Oslo. I can't lose you. Please help me understand what to do."

Little by little, Oslo instructed Ishi on how to take him apart. When it came time to detach Oslo's head, they stared at one another. This was it. Oslo wouldn't be able to guide Ishi from that point forward until he was reconstructed. Oslo bobbed his head and Ishi knew it was time. He followed Oslo's instructions and removed his head, cradling it against his chest.

"Until we meet again, my friend," he consoled the inert head.

They placed parts of Oslo around the raft, making sure it could hold the weight. Once they were sure the raft would float, the three climbed on board, also spreading their weight out by sitting away from one another. Ishi tucked the computer under his arm, hoping it worked again once they hit the island.

They couldn't risk using a motor, so they took out the attached oars and began paddling. The stars twinkled above, making it seem almost peaceful. Ishi said a small prayer and rowed as hard as he could. He was ready to take on Ms. Virginia, to find the answers to his past.

After about an hour, they could see the outline of the island. Ishi took a moment to let his arms rest and play the final details of the plan over in his head. He smiled at Bea, who smiled back. He was glad she joined them, but he worried he was risking her life.

"Thank you for coming, Bea."

She gestured with her hands, a 'you're welcome'. Ishi had been picking up some of her communication, which helped as they went over the plan. Jai paused rowing and watched them.

"What's the plan?" she asked.

"We'll row up to the other side of the island, away from the dock. We can get out there and rebuild Oslo. It will be dark and they won't be expecting us that way... I think. Once we get Oslo built, maybe the computer will work to disable the other robots."

"If it doesn't?" Jai countered.

Ishi sighed. "Then we fight like hell."

Jai grinned. "I can do that."

"I have no doubt. Do you want to tell me what happened with your mother before we do this?" Ishi asked.

"I'd be delighted. Mara and Von left to send you a message, so I slipped into the concert hall. I hid in the back behind the stage. When my mother came in, I confronted her."

"What did she say?"

"She was surprised but acted like nothing happened. She kept telling me how much she loved me. I knew she was stalling until the authorities came. I played along. She turned her back on me for a moment. I took a conductor's baton I found in the room, then jammed it into her ear. It was glorious. She flailed and tried to yank it out. It wouldn't budge. She started having a seizure and died."

Ishi didn't know what to say. What do you say to a child who is abused by their parent, then gets revenge on that parent? He watched Jai and felt a protective warmth wash over him. "I'm glad you're alright."

"Is that all you have to say? No admonishments? No shame?" Jai asked, surprised.

"It's not my place, Jai. I didn't go through what you did," Ishi confessed.

"No you didn't," Jai said, her voice hard. "But thank you, Ishi. You're my family now."

Ishi smiled at his little sister and ruffled her hair. "You are mine. Now, we need to get to this. Are you ready?"

"More than ever. I used to be sad, afraid. Not anymore. Now, I want to kick some ass," the tiny, blond girl replied.

Ishi turned to Bea. "Are you ready?"

Bea nodded and touched her eye. He'd seen the citizen-servants do that before and wondered what it meant. It seemed to be a secret sign of being there for one another, for backing each other up. He repeated the gesture to her and she grinned.

They picked up the oars and pushed as hard as they could to the land. As they neared the beach, Ishi used the oar to guide the raft where he wanted it. The raft hit the sand, making a gravelly sound. He took a deep breath. The island was quiet, lights from the big house shimmering in the distance.

Ishi climbed out and dragged the raft onto land. Bea and Jai jumped out to help and they gathered the pieces of Oslo. Ishi held his friend's head close and stared into the large round reflective eyes. A sense of courage came over him and he knew he could face the monsters who'd been tormenting them all for so long. He ran his thumb across Oslo's metal round cheek.

"It's time, Oslo."

# Chapter Thirty-Three

In the cover of darkness, the children put Oslo back together. Once his pieces were secure, Ishi wasn't sure how to bring him back to life. He pressed any buttons he could find but nothing happened. He thought about when they took Oslo apart. The robot had powered down himself. How were they supposed to power him up? Ishi slammed his fist against the ground in frustration.

"Oslo!" he yelled at the robot's still frame. Nothing happened. Ishi leaned in close, seeing if he could sense a hum or anything. However, Oslo remained silent.

Jai was standing, staring into the trees. "We can't stay here. They will find us, eventually. Do we need Oslo?"

Ishi glared at her. "Yes. We can't just leave him here, vulnerable."

Jai groaned and turned away. She seemed even more angry since killing her mother. He expected that to release her demons, but instead, it fed them. Ishi was irritated with her dismissive attitude, however, he couldn't fault her. He placed his hand on Oslo's chest, letting his hand warm the metal. He went to pull his hand away when he felt something. A low vibration.

"Bea! Come here and put your hand next to mine," Ishi exclaimed. Bea came over and placed her hand on Oslo's chest. Ishi grinned. "Do you feel that?"

Bea nodded. This caught Jai's attention and she walked over. She frowned, then leaned down and put her hand on Oslo's metal frame, as well. This seemed to increase the vibration. The children placed both hands on Oslo and the vibration spiked. Whatever they were doing, it was working. After a few minutes, the lights behind Oslo's eyes flickered and his system powered up.

Ishi couldn't explain it, but they were bringing Oslo back to life!

Oslo stirred and sat up, peering around him. "We made it to the island?"

"Yes," Ishi replied.

"Good job. It is time to finish this. Where is my computer?"

Ishi took the computer out of his pack and handed it to Oslo. "Do you think it will work?"

"There is only one way to find out," Oslo replied and turned the computer on. He rose, holding the computer in front of him. "If not, we will need to move fast and hide. Once they see us, it is all about survival."

The children bobbed their heads in unison and followed Oslo into the woods. They came to the clearing around the house and could see a line of robots guarding the structure. Oslo triggered the program to disable the robots, but nothing happened. He tried again.

"I do not know if we are able to draw the signal from this server. It may not be connected. We need to move a little closer and I will try again."

They crept closer and Oslo tried, but nothing happened. Ishi felt panic forming in his chest. They couldn't have come this far and not be able to get in there.

He set his resolve. "Let's get right up to them. If it doesn't work, then we can scatter, so maybe one of us can get inside."

Oslo nodded. "It is our only chance."

They snuck up within yards of the robots. As Oslo was preparing to activate the program, Bea accidentally stepped on a branch, which snapped under her feet. The robots' attention immediately focused on the children and they began to storm toward the group. Oslo moved in front of the children and balanced the computer in his hands. The robots descended on them, ready to fire. Oslo pressed the key and just as the robots were about to obliterate the children, they crashed to the ground. One of them lurched forward, smashing into Oslo.

The computer protecting them from the mechanical beasts flew out of Oslo's hands and shattered on the ground. Oslo scrambled for it, but when he retrieved it, the computer was broken. His eyes blazed and he faced the children.

"Go!"

The children realized the robots were recovering without the computer stopping them, rising to their feet. They began to dart toward the house, hoping to make it there before the robots got them. Ishi realized as they approached the door that Oslo wasn't with them. He spun around and saw the most horrific thing he'd witnessed yet. Two of the robots had reached Oslo and were tearing him limb from limb.

"Oslo!" Ishi cried out.

He immediately recognized his error, as the robots shifted their attention to him. They dropped Oslo's broken and battered body and came at Ishi. He bolted toward the door where Jai and Bea had made it. They screamed for him, holding the door open. Ishi stumbled and lost his cane. He wasn't going to make it.

Gathering all his strength, he thought of his mother and the boy he'd been. He needed to do this. Limping with his leg aching, Ishi pushed toward the open door As he got to the stairs, Bea reached out and pulled him inside, slamming the door behind them. It wouldn't hold the robots off for long and there were sure to be more robots inside.

Ishi bawled as they hurried down the hall, seeing Oslo being ripped apart over and over in his mind. He felt as if his own heart had been ripped from his chest. He remembered the hidden tunnels and gestured to the vent.

Bea, familiar with tunnels behind walls, unscrewed the vent and pushed Jai in, crawling in behind her. They held their hands out for Ishi, dragging him through the grate. Bea fastened it behind them and asked which way to go. Ishi got his bearings and peered around.

"This way. This goes to the children's rooms. I need to check on them first."

"First?" Jai asked.

"Yes, I need to make sure they're alright. Then, I have something I need to do."

"Ms. Virginia?"

Ishi nodded. "We also need to get to the server and see if we can deactivate the robots. I wish Timmy was here, he'd know what to do."

"Is he alive?" Jai asked.

"He was. He helped us at the Council to get out. However, without Oslo, I have no way to communicate with him," Ishi complained.

"Poor Oslo," Jai whispered, showing her softer side again. "I hate all of them."

"Me too," Ishi agreed.

They slipped down the tunnels, hearing the robots busting through the doors. Alarms went off in the building, alerting Ms. Virginia and the rest of the robots that they'd been breached. Ishi wanted to get to the children before they did, so he surged ahead.

Once they got to the first room, he could see some of the children huddled together in a corner, their eyes large with fear. It was the girls' room. He motioned to Bea.

"Can you get them into the walls? I need to check the boys' room."

Bea waved him on and began unscrewing the vent. Since she couldn't talk, Jai moved into the opening and snapped her fingers.

"Come on. You need to hide. Quickly," she instructed the girls.

The girls seemed doubtful, but then seeing it was Jai, scrambled into the vent. Ishi went on ahead, relieved the girls were hidden. He crawled through the vent to the boys's room and looked in. At first, his heart fell, thinking it was empty, then saw they were hiding under the beds. He eased the vent grate open and cleared his throat.

"Hey, it's Ishi. I need you to come here and climb in. You can hide behind the walls."

One by one, the boys slid out from under their beds. They'd shut their door and blocked it with beds but a loud banging came on the outside. The robots were there. Ishi began grabbing boys by their arms and yanking them into the opening.

"Hurry, hurry," he ordered. As the last boy was crawling through the room door flew open and the robots flooded into the room. Ishi gently closed the grate and held his breath, motioning for the boys to be silent.

The robots threw over the beds and tore apart the room. Not finding the boys, they went back into the hall, convinced the boys had hidden elsewhere. After they left, Ishi pointed for the boys to go down into the tunnel. They gathered there and Ishi brought them in a group.

"Go down the tunnel. Jai and a girl named Bea are there with the girls. I need you all to hide together until I come back. Do you understand?"

The boys nodded, then one of them, a boy named Senio, touched Ishi on the arm. "Where are you going?"

"We aren't safe. I have to get to the server room and see if I can stop the robots. We won't be free until I do. Is everyone here? Has anyone gone missing?"

Senio shook his head. "No. People came to the island today. Ms. Virginia said they were inspectors."

"Inspectors? Did they do anything? Talk to any of you?" Ishi asked, confused.

"They asked about you, Timmy, Jai, and Darius."

"Oh. Did they? Why?"

"They said Ms. Virginia accused you of killing other children. She told them that's where the missing children went," Senio explained.

Ishi was mortified. Not only had she murdered children to sell their organs, she was blaming him. His body felt prickly and he couldn't breathe. "What did you tell them?"

Senio tipped his head. "I told them you'd never do that. That you protected us."

"Did they believe you?"

"I don't think so. They said you were angry you were being sent away, so you killed children."

"I'd never do that," Ishi whispered.

"I know, Ishi. We all do, but it doesn't matter. We don't matter."

"Yes, you do!" Ishi insisted. "You are everything. Now go, before they catch you. Follow the tunnel to the left. Bea and Jai are waiting for you."

The boys disappeared into the dark as Ishi set his resolve. It was time to do what he came back to do. The thing he'd resisted when he believed there was another way.

He needed to kill Ms. Virginia.

# Chapter Thirty-Four

It was as if she'd been waiting for him all along. Ishi made it to Ms. Virginia's room and peered through the vent. Ms. Virginia was sitting in her chair at her desk, her large body kicked back as she sipped on some kind of amber liquid in a crystal glass. Ishi held his breath and thought. He had no weapons. Not even his cane. He felt through his pack and his hand landed on something unfamiliar. The tool Oslo had given Ishi to take him apart! Ishi pulled it out and turned it over in his hand. It was a long flat piece of metal with a sharp star shape at the tip. Ishi held it close to his heart and thought about Oslo.

His family.

Shoving the vent open, Ishi jumped down into the room. He wanted it to seem more threatening, but his twisted leg buckled on impact, pitching Ishi forward. He reached out and grasped Ms. Virginia's desk, righting himself.

She snorted and took a sip of the liquid. "Smooth."

Ishi clutched the tool, waving it out in front of him. "I hate you."

Ms. Virginia roared with laughter. "So?"

That threw Ishi off. He didn't know what he was expecting confronting her, but it wasn't that. His hands trembled as he swallowed dryly. "You are evil."

Ms. Virginia shrugged. "It has served me well. So, what exactly are you planning to do here? Leap over the table and stab me with that little thing?"

Ishi didn't like how she wasn't afraid. Not even not afraid, she was challenging him. He wanted to see her beg for her life. That wasn't happening.

"Who was my mother?"

Ms. Virginia's eyebrows raised and she leaned forward. "Really? That's what you want to know? She was a wretch. Wasting air. Breeding. When you got injured and taken away from her, she tried to get you back. Your father disappeared shortly after, likely for causing waves. Records say he was imprisoned and died in there. You were her youngest. I don't know what happened to the other children but your mother killed herself after you were taken. Trash taking itself out."

Rage surged through Ishi. She was so callous and flippant about him losing his whole family. "Why are you even here? How are you in charge of this island?"

Ms. Virginia yawned. "Better hurry up with this, I'm bored. My family comes from good blood. I was offered this island as an entitlement. I see it as a punishment. I hate children."

Ishi couldn't stop his shaking. He was scared, he was angry, he was at the end of his rope. His family was gone, there would be no happy reunion. All of a sudden, he understood Jai's rage, her commitment to ending the person who took her dreams of a family away. Surprising even himself, Ishi leapt on the desk and kicked the glass out of Ms. Virginia's hands. If she was shocked, she didn't show it. She leaned back, an amused expression on her face. That was it. The final straw.

Ishi jumped on top of her and impaled her in the eye with the tool. He stabbed her over and over. She didn't even seem to fight back. He kept going until his arm ached and he heard robot steps coming down the hall. Ishi pushed himself off the massive, very bloody, very dead body. It was as if she wanted him to do it all along.

Seoul, the toad, gazed unperturbed from the corner of the desk, licking his eyes every few seconds. Ishi stared at the toad, remembering how Ms. Virginia made him and the other children drink the substance Seoul secreted. It made them see terrible things, scary visions. Ishi didn't blame the creature and opened the window to let it go. The toad stared for a moment, then hopped through the window and disappeared out of view.

Ishi made it back to vent and pulled himself up through it. As he dragged his body into the dark space, the robots came through the door and stared at Ms. Virginia. Ishi observed from behind the grate. They didn't rush to help or even seem to care. They simply rotated and walked out of the room. They felt no indignation at her murder.

Ishi drew his knees to his chest and sobbed. For Nora. For Oslo. For the children who'd disappeared. He'd killed Ms. Virginia, but he couldn't bring any of them back. He made his way down the tunnels until he found Bea, Jai, and the rest of the children. They swarmed around him and Jai met his eyes.

"Satisfying, isn't it?"

He nodded, wiping blood off his face. "It was."

They moved through the walls until it opened into a utility room. Everyone spread out and lay down, exhausted. The other children asked about what happened, about the mainland. Ishi told them what he could, then closed his eyes. They weren't done yet. The robots were still roaming the building, searching for them. They did seem less adamant now that Ms. Virginia was dead, but Ishi couldn't take any chances. He dozed off and dreamed about Oslo.

The sun was up when he woke and the children were complaining of being hungry. Bea and Ishi went back through the hidden halls to the kitchen and grabbed whatever food was in there. It wasn't much. Clearly, Ms. Virginia wasn't planning on the children surviving. They went to Ms. Virginia's room and paused. Bea stared at the mangled body, then glanced at Ishi. She pointed at him and he nodded. She tipped her head in understanding and opened the grate.

They raided the space, stuffing everything edible they could find into their packs. When they got back to the children, they feasted. By nightfall, Ishi knew they needed to figure out how to get out and disable the robots. He was aware of where the server was but there was no way there without going through the halls. He helped the children bed down and drew Bea and Jai aside.

"Tomorrow we need to find a way to finish this."

They agreed but no one had any ideas. Ishi told them to sleep on it and rested in a corner. He was surprised as he felt his eyes get heavy.

Tomorrow.

The next morning, they told the children their plan. Bea would stay with the children, while Jai and Ishi would find a way to the server room. They ate a light breakfast and Ishi and Jai went into the wall tunnels to get as far as they could. The last stretch was an open hall. Once they got to the last vent, Ishi heard a strange sound. It sounded like yelling, like a roar of people. He frowned and slipped out into the hall, which was devoid of robots. The noise was coming from outside. Jai followed him and they crept to the closest window.

What they saw froze them in place.

Out on the lawn, a vicious battle was raging. Raiders and robots fighting it out. The children stared in amazement. Then Ishi realized they had a chance to get to the computers He grabbed Jai by the arm.

"Quick! While they are preoccupied."

They ran down the hall to the server room and went inside. Ishi searched for a lock but there wasn't one. They needed to get it done as quickly as possible. He remembered they couldn't destroy the computers, they had to disable the robots. He opened the computer and stared at the screen. What was it again? What had Timmy told him?

He went through the steps from memory, not knowing if it worked until a loud shout of celebration went up outside. Jai and Ishi looked at each other, then ran to the closest window. The robots were collapsing into heaps on the ground.

It worked!

"Jai, go tell the children they can come out!" Ishi yelled, a sense of power washing over him.

She hurried down the hall and within minutes, children and Raiders were flowing into the halls. Adults were approaching children and taking them under their wings. Ishi gazed at the scene, still hurting for Oslo. He should be there.

He stumbled through the crowd of people when he spied a familiar face. Mara! He ran up and threw his arms around her. Von came around the corner with a big grin. Mara stepped back.

"We thought you could use some help," she whispered.

"Thank you, Mara! We did it. Well, sort of. They destroyed Oslo and we only disabled the robots. We need to reprogram them, but I don't know how," Ishi replied.

"Oh? I may just have what you need," Mara said, a twinkle in her eyes.

"What?" Ishi asked.

Von had disappeared, then come back around the corner, hiding something behind his back. Not something, someone... or two. He stepped aside and Ishi fell to his knees, his arms outstretched.

Timmy and Dari darted to him with their hands clasped to each other's, knocking Ishi over and creating a pile of boys on the ground. Ishi held on so tight, they began to wriggle away.

"Ishi, you're squeezing us!" Dari said, laughing.

They all sat up and Ishi stared in amazement. Timmy was breathing better and had color in his cheeks. Ishi touched the boys to make sure they were real.

Timmy giggled. "So, let's get these robots on our side."

"Can you?" Ishi asked.

Mara came over. "He sure can. The Raiders brought him to the mainland after you left. He reprogrammed the robots there and they helped the citizen-servants defeat the elite. We still have a ways to go but when we came here, we were getting the upper hand. We need Timmy's all over the world."

"Well, let's start here," Ishi replied. "Timmy, follow me to the server room, and let's get these metal monsters on our side."

They went to the computer room and within minutes, Timmy had the robots reprogrammed and waking up. The Raiders went to each robot and welcomed them to their new life and purpose. Even the robots seemed happier with the change, following the Raiders to the house.

Ishi was so proud of his little brother but crushed about Oslo. He told Timmy what happened to Oslo and how their robot friend had stood by them until the very end. Saying the words out loud hurt Ishi's heart, but he knew he'd carry Oslo with him forever. Timmy was quiet, then got up and walked out of the room.

Ishi went after him, calling out, "Timmy, where are you going?"

Timmy turned with an impish grin. "Are you taking me to Oslo or what?"

# Family

Oslo's eyes focused around him and he saw everyone he loved watching him intently. He sat up, staring at his body. It was different. No longer mismatched and in pieces. He clenched his new fingers together and turned his head. His legs were the same length and his feet matched.

Oslo saw Ishi and tipped his head. "How?"

Ishi pointed to Oslo's other side. The robot rotated and saw Timmy standing by him, his face beaming with pride. Oslo couldn't believe it. "Timmy! You are here."

Timmy smiled. "I am here. We all are. I scavenged new parts for you."

Oslo gazed at the children, then saw Mara and Von. Mara knelt by him. "We did it. We're changing things. The robots everywhere are being reprogrammed, thanks to Timmy developing instructions. Children are being reunited with their families. The Service is being overthrown. We have a long way to go, but it's happening."

Oslo looked at Ishi. "Ms. Virginia?"

"Dead," the boy, who was now becoming a man, answered without shame.

"Are you staying on the island?" Oslo asked.

Ishi nodded. "My family is gone. This is my family now. It always was. The island has been taken back and is now a sanctuary for children without families. One of many."

"You did it," Oslo said with pride.

Ishi shook his head. "No, *we* did it. I love you, Oslo. I couldn't have done this without you. Oh, and we have new family members here on the island."

Oslo tipped his head, then saw Pashmira and the other surviving Maboni step forward. Pashmira put her arm over Ishi's shoulder. "Ishi has welcomed us back to the island and we have decided to be each other's people. Ishi is my son, I am his mother now. All of the children left here have adopted parents with the Maboni. Some were able to be returned to their families, but the rest have a family here, now. We will always love and honor those we have lost, but it's time to embrace our future. I'm so glad to see you again, Oslo, my friend."

Jai came forward, leading Zelai by the hand. "Zelai is my mommy, now. She is teaching me her ways. Like Gapul."

Oslo got up and hugged Jai and Zelia. He faced Ishi, and Pashmira, his eyes glowing with emotion.

Ishi reached out and touched Oslo's chest, letting his fingers remain on the cool metal. "Timmy even gave you a mechanical heart to match your soul one."

Oslo placed his hand on his metal core, over Ishi's hand, and nodded. "You are the blood of my heart."

"Oh, and look," Ishi said. "Timmy made me a leg brace out of your old parts he didn't need to restore you. I can walk without a cane."

"What is next?" Oslo asked.

"We make a world where humans and robots of all kinds can live together and honor all differences," Pashmira replied with a soft smile.

Ishi shrugged. "Now, we change the world."

# Acknowledgments

Thank you to Bee at sillyclub.xyz for her amazing art and patience getting the idea to fruition. Thank you to Dino Hicks for your awesome feedback and support.

Thank you to my soul sister, Lizzy, for being an unending cheerleader and friend. Thank you to my family for understanding when I am buried in my work and less than attentive.

Thank you to all the readers who believe in what I am creating and reminding me I am doing something important.

# Books by the Author

Do Over

We Don't Matter

Prick of the Needle

Through the Surface

Trigger Point

Carrying the Dead

Catch the Earth

In Dreams, We Fly

Stitched Together

By the Dimming Light

Expectation of Pain

Please visit my website for upcoming books and news:

authorjulietrose.com

Made in the USA
Columbia, SC
27 October 2024

45138223R00159